Janie May Phillips

Last Chances: Deserted Island

AF204990

Janie May Phillips

Last Chances: Deserted Island

JustFiction Edition

Impressum/Imprint (nur für Deutschland/only for Germany)
Bibliografische Information der Deutschen Nationalbibliothek: Die Deutsche Nationalbibliothek verzeichnet diese Publikation in der Deutschen Nationalbibliografie; detaillierte bibliografische Daten sind im Internet über http://dnb.d-nb.de abrufbar.
Alle in diesem Buch genannten Marken und Produktnamen unterliegen warenzeichen-, marken- oder patentrechtlichem Schutz bzw. sind Warenzeichen oder eingetragene Warenzeichen der jeweiligen Inhaber. Die Wiedergabe von Marken, Produktnamen, Gebrauchsnamen, Handelsnamen, Warenbezeichnungen u.s.w. in diesem Werk berechtigt auch ohne besondere Kennzeichnung nicht zu der Annahme, dass solche Namen im Sinne der Warenzeichen- und Markenschutzgesetzgebung als frei zu betrachten wären und daher von jedermann benutzt werden dürften.

Coverbild: www.ingimage.com

Verlag: JustFiction! Edition ist ein Imprint der
LAP LAMBERT Academic Publishing GmbH & Co. KG
Heinrich-Böcking-Str. 6-8, 66121 Saarbrücken, Deutschland
Telefon +49 681 37 20 310, Telefax +49 681 37 20 310-9
Email: info@justfiction-edition.com

Herstellung in Deutschland:
Schaltungsdienst Lange o.H.G., Berlin
Books on Demand GmbH, Norderstedt
Reha GmbH, Saarbrücken
Amazon Distribution GmbH, Leipzig
ISBN: 978-3-8454-4559-5

Imprint (only for USA, GB)
Bibliographic information published by the Deutsche Nationalbibliothek: The Deutsche Nationalbibliothek lists this publication in the Deutsche Nationalbibliografie; detailed bibliographic data are available in the Internet at http://dnb.d-nb.de.
Any brand names and product names mentioned in this book are subject to trademark, brand or patent protection and are trademarks or registered trademarks of their respective holders. The use of brand names, product names, common names, trade names, product descriptions etc. even without a particular marking in this works is in no way to be construed to mean that such names may be regarded as unrestricted in respect of trademark and brand protection legislation and could thus be used by anyone.

Cover image: www.ingimage.com

Publisher: JustFiction! Edition
is an imprint of the publishing house
LAP LAMBERT Academic Publishing GmbH & Co. KG
Heinrich-Böcking-Str. 6-8, 66121 Saarbrücken, Germany
Phone +49 681 37 20 310, Fax +49 681 37 20 310-9
Email: info@justfiction-edition.com

Printed in the U.S.A.
Printed in the U.K. by (see last page)
ISBN: 978-3-8454-4559-5

Deserted Island

Every year Chrys, her two sisters and her two best friends went somewhere wild and new, they were adventurous to say the least. This year they decided to go to a quaint little island no one could really pronounce the name of.

Chrys and her little twin sisters Marianne and Marybeth's parents are billionaires so they pretty much get to do whatever they want to. Their father's a famous defense attorney to the rich and famous. Their mother's a real-estate agent, whose father made a substantial amount as an inventor. So neither her mother nor her father was around much leaving Chrys to set the rules. It hadn't always been easy, but she knew how privileged she was so she never complained.

Her best friend Frank was vastly rich too, but, her other best friend Kalvin wasn't though. He'd had a hard life and been through some hard times. His father was an abusive drunk and that was pretty much all she knew about him, he didn't talk about his past very often.

Nonetheless, they all packed up and headed to the local dock. They were taking the private cargo jet from their home to the island. They went this way so they could take their jeep. Chrys wanted to rough it on this little island just outside the Caribbean that hadn't been developed for the most part; it was more of a native island. Little did she know she would never see that island...

"Kal," Chrys called "did you bring the oil for the lamps?" When she said rough it, she meant it.

"Yeah, I got 'em" he said quietly.

"What's wrong?" Chrys asked him, putting her slender hand on his shoulder.

Her sisters and Frank had seen the romance budding for about a year now, when their trip was originally planned for. They were going to go two years ago and the year after, but Chrys got immensely sick and they couldn't expose her to the weather. She had thought she had the flu so she went to the doctors and eventually diagnosed with leukemia. She'd been in remission for about eight months now, but her immune system wasn't completely there. She didn't care, though she was going anyway.

"Nothin', just- nothin'" he mumbled tossing the stuff onto the jeep.

"Kal, you can tell me" seventeen-year-old Chrys said her big brown eyes shimmering.

"Should you be going?" he asked and she laughed

"I'm fine" she stated and attempted to pull herself up on top of the pile of stuff in the jeep. It wasn't big enough for all five of them so Kal volunteered to ride with her back there. Chrys was frugal with money, even though they had so much to spend; she'd only rented a cargo plane with room for the pilot and the car so they had to ride in it still. You could see the strain in her face to pull herself two feet up she was so weak.

"Here" Kalvin said climbing up and grabbing her hand to pull her up "I got ya"

"Thanks" she said smiling "Oh! Crap, Bethy did you grab the bag of my meds?"

Kalvin cringed and looked hard at Marybeth. He was big, and intimidating looking, in an attractive sort of way, and he could be if pushed the wrong way, except with Chrys. Ever since he met her, she couldn't do a thing wrong in his eyes.

"Yeah, it's back there" eleven-year-old Marybeth told her

"Thanks" Chrys replied.

"Here, Chrys" Marianne said handing her a blanket and sweatshirt.

2

"Thanks" Chrys mumbled she was sensitive about her illness. At one point, she was so close to death they thought she wouldn't come back, but she's a fighter.

****

Marybeth turned around and held a camera up to Chrys and Kalvin. She was their resident photographer. Chrys smiled and leaned her head on Kalvin. Who in return smiled and put his arm on her shoulder.

"Chrys and Kalvin sitting in a tree K-I-S-S-I-N-G" Frank teased and Chrys stuck her tongue out at him. The pale white tongue reminded them all of how this could be their last chance to spend with her. The doctors had said they'd never seen such an amazing recovery. But, she wasn't out of the water, yet. According to the doctors with a fighting spirit like hers, it wouldn't surprise them if she fought to live harder than anyone they'd ever seen. They cautioned however, not to put her through too much stress. They made a point not to get their hopes up too high, because even if she seems better it doesn't mean she is.

****

Chrys'd fallen asleep on Kal's lap and he just looked at her, with his hand on her shoulder. By the time, the plane circled the island to land, the pilot got worried when he couldn't see a landing spot. Since the island was relatively uninhabited and not very well known he had never flown there before, therefore wasn't quite sure of what it looked like. He didn't want to alarm his young passengers, and soon he found an open spot and got ready to land. He figured an undeveloped island would only have and open field or strip of land. There was no answer on the radio, but then again it was called undeveloped for a reason, and his coordinates said that this was the island, so he decided not to worry anymore. But in the back of his head, there was an inclination that he'd missed something, or got it wrong. But the young passengers just went on with themselves...

Kalvin faded back into memories as he looked at her sleeping...

****

"You know, without her I'd probably be dead and now she's dying and there's nothing I can do." He said to Marianne as they stood outside her hospital room.

3

"She'll be fine, she always is," said the naive Marybeth. "Just ask her...she'll tell you"...

****

He came back from the memories before the bad parts every time he drifted off. He just looked off into the ocean, as they circled to land one more time.

Frank said, "Dude, she'll get better; she's got the best doctors"

"It's *not about money*, life'll do whatever it wants." Nineteen-year old Kalvin told him "*In life, there are some things money just can't buy*"

"She hasn't slept like that for weeks," Marianne said quietly trying to get them to leave the subject alone. She wouldn't say so in her quite ways but she hated the subject absolutely despised it.

Chrys sat up then.

"Speak of the devil" eighteen-year-old Frank laughed.

"Where are we?" Chrys asked rubbing her eyes.

"Over the island." Frank said

"No dip Sherlock" She said annoyed, she had been listening to the last few lines of their conversation and she hated it, it made her really mad "I mean how close?"

"Seconds" Kal said quietly

"Cool, is anyone else really bored?" she asked popping the top off a box of animal crackers.

"Yeah, I am" Marybeth said

"You're always bored." Marianne added

"No I'm not you never do anything fun!" Marybeth argued

"Guys...guys...guys!" Chrys screamed as suddenly their plane was sent into a tailspin. They flew around as the pilots tried to get control of the plane. Even the pilots weren't sure what was going on. It was a few minutes before they got control back but

4

by then it was too late. They were too low to pull back up, and all that was below was woods. They flew until they found a patch of land, to land in. They still thought they were on the small little island, just a bit off their intended destination. They decided, with no other real option, that this was good enough. They explained to their young passengers what had happened and everything seemed fine. From their calculations, they were only a couple miles off.

The plane flew off then. What they didn't know was that the pilots had made a terrible error in their original calculations. There shouldn't have even been an island there but there was. They were headed to IcBan the town where they were to meet their tour guides and head off to their cabin. They drove up onto the dirt road and hopped off. Chrys's big brown eyes stared in amazement at the vast amount of trees. Her light brown hair slapping her face in the wind.

"Whoa" she said her words getting lost in the wind.

Meztal and Mora were supposed to be their tour guides; no one could find Meztal or Mora. They drove around and around and they couldn't find anyone. Something was very wrong. They finally found a path that lead over a hill, they thought maybe the town was on the other side of the hill and they just didn't get the right directions. Their jeep puttered to the top of the hill and what they saw on the other side amazed them. A river of mud ran down the hill to a pool. They tried to back up but it was too late, they slid down the hill and into the mud pit in a swoosh of motion.

The twins screamed and Chrys grabbed onto Kalvins' sleeve. When they came to a stop in the mud hole Kalvin and Frank scrambled out and helped the girls out. They ran back as the jeep sunk to the bottom. It wasn't very deep, but all their stuff was in it including Chrys's medicine.

"I can go for about three days before it will hit me hard" she said quietly, "But, now we have to find if there are any people on this island."

"No, shelter first, people later. It's about dark and I don't know what animals are on this island, but, I ain't about to stick around and find out." Kalvin said walking towards a wooded hill.

"This way" he said leading them towards the hill to look for shelter for the night.

The cave was pushed into the back of the mountain with trampled trees hanging in front of it. Kalvin and Frank helped Chrys and the girls up the mountain. They checked the cave and when it was empty they crawled, exhausted, inside of it. They made a plan to go tomorrow to look for help and if they couldn't find any they would make this home.

They didn't find help. Over the course of the whole next day and part of the night, they walked the island to every border and there was no one there. Only Kalvin and Frank went out for the couple of hours of the night. They decided they had to dig their supplies out of the mud hole they sunk it in. They surveyed the area and found they would need a lever and pulley system to get it out. They were all thankful that Kalvin and Frank took that survival class their sophomore/freshman year.

"Okay, I think since Chrys needs her meds we dig it out first" Kalvin suggested

"No, I have one more day" Chrys said, "We need a place to stay, I've seen movies like this, and we could be here for a *very* long time."

"Okay, well, what do we need to survive?" Marybeth asked

"Water, and food" Marianne said quietly

"Shelter and clothes" Frank added in, "Protection from wild animals"

"Well, okay let's put up shelter near a clean source of water. Then go from there on the list." Chrys suggested

"Okay, let's go" Kalvin said uneasily

"Protection from wild animals would be up high, right?" Frank asked

"I would think so." Kalvin answered

"So in a really strong tree? Or...or on a ledge or something" Marybeth asked

"I think we should be like the Swiss Family Robinson©" Marianne said from the back, prompting them to look at her. It was surprising to hear they were twins if you didn't know, they nearly looked nothing alike. The only things they had in common was their height, face shape and eyes; they had the most gorgeous baby blue eyes. Marybeth was the blonde bombshell; shoulder length blonde hair. Marianne on the other hand was a red head with freckles. Their personalities were as different as their looks. Marybeth was loud and confident, while Marianne is shy and quiet. Truthfully, they were as different as night and day.

"You read that to us once, do you remember?" she asked Chrys

"Yeah, when you guys were in the hospital getting your tonsils taken out!" Chrys said

"Anyway" Marybeth said impatiently

"Anyway" Marianne mocked, "They had more than one hut, for hard weather and easy weather"

"Oh, I get it so you're saying that we should too" Chrys said looking at the people "what do ya think?"

"I think we should make one that's for easy and hard weather" Frank said, "We could be here for a while so we should make it comfortable but strong"

"That's sound really smart; I think we should devise a plan first" Chrys started "You know, like a layout things with like supplies and stuff."

"Sounds good, um we can use the cave rock to draw it with stones!" Frank said and they raced back to the cave to get started

"Okay let's see," Chrys started "Um; well we'll need a really tall big tree"

"Right and we'll need bunch of wood." Kalvin said thinking of the house itself

"No, we don't have nails or hammers, something we can tie with like reeds or something" Frank corrected him

"Okay, well that means water, right?" Marianne asked

"Right, um, so I guess we'll need to start gathering these things," Chrys said walking to the cave door and seeing where the sun was in the sky. "I'd guess we have about five hours 'til the sun sets"

"Well that should give us about enough time to find a good tree." Marybeth said heading down the hill

"Wait! Beth! Beth, you have to wait for them!" Marianne yelled running after her

"Grab something to mark the tree with, we won't have time to start today, I have to go get them." Chrys said following the twins

"Wait, mark it with what?" Frank yelled after her

"Be creative!" she yelled back

"Um, what about a rock?" Kalvin asked

"To do what with?" Frank asked, "Smash against the tree?"

"No dip wad, cut into the tree." Kalvin said grabbing a rock, and running down the hill

"Hey, Grace don't hurt yourself, because I ain't digging out the first aid kit today!" Chrys teased as Frank nearly fell running down the hill

"Shut up!" he said

"Okay where do you want to start?" Marybeth asked

"Um, well, I guess we could split up and when we find something mark it and tomorrow we'll decide which one is the best" Chrys suggested

"Sounds good to me, so how are we gonna split up?" Frank asked

"Well there are five of us and I don't want them going without one of you," Chrys said "so one of you can go with them and one with me?"

"Okay, sounds good, who's going with them?" Kalvin asked

"I will" Frank volunteered, "Okay, let's go this way"

"Okay, looks like it's just you and me" Chrys said smiling as she slid her arm through his

"Sure is" he smiled as they walked west and Frank and the twins walked east.

They walked for about three hours without any luck before they finally stumbled upon a tree that seemed suitable to live in. They decided to measure it around with their arms and see if it seemed strong enough to hold everything. It turned out that it was four arms lengths around for Kalvin and five for Chrys. It had to be about one hundred feet high at the top and since it was similar to an oak tree the smallest it got was about half an arm's length around.

"It looks good to me!" Kalvin said as he slid the rock over the bark again and again and again until a large R was cut into it.

"R?" Chrys asked

"Robinson. You know like <u>Swiss Family Robinson</u>©." Kalvin said

"Oh that's so cute!" Chrys said as they turned around and walked hastily back toward the cave

"Oh, you know what we should do, with the cave, since it's not that far of a walk?" Kalvin blurted out randomly, they'd gone in all different directions since they started before hand.

"No, what?" Chrys asked, looking up with her big brown eyes

"Store food." Kalvin explained "You know, cause in all reality we're not expected back for another month and then they'll search in the Caribbean they won't even think to look here I bet no one's ever seen it before. Like I don't know, what even happened it's like the pilots didn't even see it then they just landed! I mean I doubt that's what happened but, yeah."

"Weird" Chrys said simply "But, yeah"

They walked back to the cave as fast as they could but it was still dark when they got back. Marianne was waiting at the door for them. She hugged Chrys as they walked in; Chrys put her arm around Annie as they sat down in the cave.

"Chrys" Marianne started "Are we ever gonna get off this island?"

"I don't know" Chrys said "but whatever happens we'll be fine. We know everything we need to know and what we don't know we'll figure out"

"Yeah, but, what happens if they never find us, you'll run out of your medicine!" Marianne cried

Kalvin shot a glance at Frank, he'd never thought of it. Frank shook his head no, like everything will be fine. It was very clear that Kalvin had fallen hard for her.

"That won't happen, don't worry" she said putting her arm over her baby sisters shoulder and pulling her into a hug. Chrys rubbed Marianne's shoulders and hair.

"It'll be just fine" she kissed her sisters head as Marianne clung to her.

"Chrys" Kalvin said quietly and she turned around to look at him, and Marianne walked away "She-she's right you know, what happens when you run out?"

Chrys shrugged and looked at him with big eyes, big shaking eyes. Kalvin walked over to her and wrapped his arms around her shoulders. She buried her face in his chest, her hands resting on his shoulder blades, arms under his.

She whispered low enough so her sisters couldn't hear "I'm scared"

"Don't be," he whispered, "You'll be just fine, I'll make sure of it"

"Do you wanna take a walk?" she whispered into his chest

He laughed, and kissed the top of her head. He froze; he hadn't meant to do that, at least not then. But, she didn't seem to mind, she just pulled in tighter. Kalvin looked over to Frank and Frank motioned to go. Frank didn't mean it in the exact way Kal took it, but either way he listened.

"Sure thing" Kalvin said and Chrys let go, only keeping the right half of her body latched onto him. As they walked in the moonlight, Chrys smiled up at Kalvin.

"Hey" he whispered "Chrys you can tell me, what's gonna happen. I won't tell them I promise"

"Okay, well I'll be fine but my system will have to like- it's like, like being off drugs you have to recover. You know?" she said her voice shaking

"Yeah" he said, "I get it"

"Like withdrawal" she said quietly "So long as I don't relapse I'll be fine"

"Relapse?" he asked the sudden thought of what had seen her go through floated into his mind "Y-you can relapse?"

"Oh, I doubt I will" she said seeing how white his face got every time someone talked about her dying or being sick. "I'll be fine don't worry" It always seemed out of place to her, how white he got. He'd been through so much in his life and yet the thought of losing her terrified him. To her it never quite made sense.

"You don't sound too sure" he whispered

"You don't need to worry, you have Frank and Beth and Anne have our parents, sometime. So who'd miss me?"

"Who'd miss you? You're the whole thing; without you those girls wouldn't be who they are you practically raised them. And Frank, well he's Frank." Kalvin trailed off

"And you..." she said softly "You'd be just fine. I know you would you'd most likely not be here because that's my fault, but, wherever you'd be you'd be great at it."

"Yeah, right, you're the only reason I'm still alive, I'd be dead or on drugs and close to dead" he wrapped his arms around her again and kissed the top of her head. He let go and they walked back to the cave.

"Kal," she whispered softly

"Yeah?" he asked her as she looked up at him with big eyes

"Nothing" she said taking his hand as they walked back to the cave "Are we ever gonna get outta here?"

"Of course, and when we do you can buy the island and we can come back every year." He told her smiling as she let go of his hand and walked into the cave

"Our own little oasis" she said smiling

"God! Next time don't forget to tell me you're gonna be gone for three days!" Frank whispered

"Yes, mom" Kalvin snickered and Frank punched his arm

Marianne sat up then "Chrys?"

"Yeah, go back to sleep"

"No, Chrys, wait we have to get a house"

"Tomorrow" Chrys told her sitting next to her. Marianne put her head in Chrys's lap and Chrys stroked her hair.

Sometime in the middle of the night Chrys sat up having trouble breathing, she was cold and hot at the same time. She tried to stand but was too weak. She knew this was coming the day before but hid it as best as she could. She hated this feeling; she had it for about a week every time they switched her meds because they had to get the others out of her system because they were so potent. She tried to sleep but she just couldn't. So at what she guessed was near morning she woke Kalvin and Frank up.

"Guys, guys" she coughed "Wake up!"

"What?" Frank moaned

"Withdrawal" she stated simply, "we have to dig the stuff out today before it gets any worse"

"Okay" they said standing up and slipping out the door

She sat there waiting for them when she heard the rumbled of the the thunder she knew they weren't going to be able to get it out today. She mustered up the strength to stand near the door, it was still early and the twins were still sleeping. They came running up the hill, covered in mud and empty handed.

"S-Sorry it started raining and the mud came down harder and faster, but the good news is the mud underneath near the top of our car hardened. I don't know how far it's hard but it'll be easier to dig, right?" Kalvin asked and she coughed. Her eyes were red; she'd never had it set in so fast before.

"We'll go back when it stops raining again, ok?" Frank asked

She nodded and slid to the floor near the door. She felt like sleeping for hours on end. Kalvin sat near her and she leaned over on him.

"Sleep" she whispered, he thought she meant that he should sleep, but she meant she was going to sleep for a long time. And she did, for nearly two days she slept on and off. They moved her to a bed they made in the corner. And waited, they'd never seen it rain for that long before.

Just as the rain began to die down Chrys woke up and stayed awake.

"I'm so hungry," Chrys moaned as she leaned against the cave wall. Kalvin reached over and rubbed her hand. It'd been six or more days since she last had her medication. They didn't exactly know.

"We're all hungry!" Marybeth snapped, "No one's eaten yet, we can't eat until it stops raining!"

"Beth, she's sick, she probably needs food more than we do!" Marianne scolded her.

"Guys, shut up!" Frank said holding his hand up from the cave door "I think I hear something."

"What?" Kalvin whispered and the loud growling of a large cat rang through the cave. Chrys gasped and grabbed at his hand.

She whispered, "Get it, Kal" with big eyes

"Shh" he said pulling her into his arms and carrying her back into her corner. She'd been running a fever and she wasn't sure of what she was saying. Their jeep was still buried so she hadn't had her medicine.

"Okay, it's decided we're leaving and living in the hut! I don't care if it's done; I'm not living here one more second!" Marybeth cried

"Shh" Marianne said, "we'll leave tomorrow. We'll have to dig our stuff out, too, so that will get Chrys her meds."

"I'm so sick of you telling me to shhhh!" Marybeth snapped

"Marybeth, stop!" Kalvin said, "This isn't helping anyone! If we can't stick together, we'll never get out of this alive! So, stop, in order to make it through this you two have to pull yourselves together do you understand me!?"

"Yes" they mumbled in unison

"Good, now we have a lot of work to do and one of you is staying here with her and the other is coming with us to dig the jeep out, so who's gonna work in the mud?" Kalvin asked

They looked at each other and Marybeth went to open her mouth when Marianne spoke up "I'll go with you"

"What?" Marybeth asked, "You hate mud!"

"I know, but I need to go out and do something." She said quietly

"Okay, fair enough let's go" Frank said as they left

They walked down to the mud pit, which was about a twenty-minute walk. Once they got there, they saw that it had completely encased the jeep. Even if he didn't say, anything Kalvin worried that they'd lost everything.

"Um, how-how are we gonna do this?" Marianne asked looking at the giant mud pit.

"I have no idea" Frank answered "I guess were gonna have to jump in and see how far down it goes and then see if we can get anything out

"Um okay but I'm like 4 foot 11" Marianne asked

"Um, then you can put the stuff in a pile and like wipe the mud off of it." Kal answered

"Okay..." she said skeptically

Frank and Kalvin looked at each other as they slowly walked into the mud. When it got up to their chest Frank ducked under to see if he could find the Jeep in the muck. Kalvin followed and for half an hour, they did this up-and-down, up-and-down, up-and-down, over-and-over and over-and-over. Finally, Frank came up and shouted:

"Found it!" his whole body caked in mud

"Yes!" Marianne jumped up and down with joy.

When Kalvin came up Frank and him went back down and showed him where he found it. They would later found out that it was about ten feet down.

Kalvin came up brought a bag with him it, eventually they'd brought up about five or six bags and they weren't even sure if they were half done or not. They kept at it until the sun was near set. Kalvin and Frank set at lugging the big things up the hill while

Marianne and Marybeth ran up and down with the small things. They didn't have a lot with them because the plane they had was so small; they'd only rented it under Chrys's dad's name. They searched feverously through the stuff they'd gotten for her medication praying the mud hadn't ruined it.

"I've got it!" Kalvin yelled when he opened the bag. He ran over to her and pulled all of the stuff out "Here- here take it"

She reached over and took the huge bottle of pills, tried to twist the cap off but was too weak. Anxiously Kalvin picked it up and nearly ripped the cap off. She reached in and took two pills out, swallowed them and then threw them back up.

She looked up at him and said, "Have to have two" and he dumped two more in her hand

She took those and nearly threw them up too, but, he tipped her head back and she kept them down. She laid back down after that and slept through the night. They went through the things they'd brought up and tried to see what they had left in the mud. They also tried to come up with a plan to get the Jeep out of the mud hole. Obviously they weren't going to get it out the same way they got the stuff out it was way too heavy for that. They tried to think of something strong enough to pull it out with that wouldn't break, but they soon moved on from that.

"Okay, we've got my suitcase, Beth's suitcase, one box of food- with no way to cook it, one of blankets and pillows & stuff, Kalvins suitcase, another box of water & stuff, and um, Chrys's medicine bag" Marianne whispered

"Okay well tomorrow we'll just go do the same thing tomorrow until all the stuff is out" Frank said

"But I thought tomorrow we were moving out?" Marybeth asked

"Well then we'll have to do that the next day" Kalvin passed her off and that only made her angrier

"No, you said tomorrow!" she protested

"Marybeth stop!" Marianne ordered, she tended to take control of her sister when she got like this

"But-" she started

"Stop!" Chrys said firmly from the corner, they didn't think she was listening. She wasn't really sure of what she was saying; she'd just woken up and was still a little groggy.

They all froze where they were, she didn't say another word. Eventually they just went on with it, well Marianne did and everyone else seemed to follow.

"We need to get everything out and we can worry about cleaning it later," Marianne told them

"We also need to move as soon as possible." Marybeth whispered

Marianne stared at her and said, "We need to build when we're done with getting the stuff out. Then once the basic structure is built we can move in and work from there."

"Sounds good to me" Chrys agreed she was still groggy but the medicine had helped a little.

They looked over at her and she was just looking at them "I want to help" she whispered softly

"Okay" Kalvin told her and she smiled weakly and sat up

"We brought" she coughed "one to two suitcases each and at least ten boxes of food and water and other stuff. So total" cough "that's at least fifteen boxes, at most," deep breath "twenty. How many do we have?"

"Seven-ish" Marianne said

Chrys sighed "We're not making progress" she coughed and decided on what they needed to do "Tomorrow the guys are gonna go and dig the rest out, bright-" she coughed "And early, then I'll go looking for water, cause we're not gonna have enough." She wheezed, looking for breath.

Kalvin got up and went over to her, she grabbed onto his arm until she could talk again. "Thanks, anyway we're not going fast enough, and I know that it's because I was sick, but, I'm better so we need to get our stuff out and build the house soon, or we're gonna die. So tomorrow the girls are gonna find material to build with and I'm gonna find water or a place where I think that there's water. And you guys get the stuff out and start to clean it as best as we can we need to get moving." She struggled to say that without stopping but she seemed determined as if it would prove that she was okay now, even though it was obvious she wasn't. It took a couple minutes to catch her breath.

Kalvin nodded, and she lay back against the wall listening to them talk and bicker for the rest of the night. Kalvin sat by her and they laughed at the twins arguing and Frank trying to be the referee.

"They do this all the time." Chrys whispered and Kalvin laughed

"No wonder" he commented.

"Why?" Chrys asked.

"Well, they're twins so people expect them to be alike, but, they're two separate people."

"Sounds like you would know" she looked at him, even though she'd know him for over two years now, since she was diagnosed she knew little about his past.

"I would" he looked at her "I had a twin once"

"Had?" she looked up at him then.

"Had. You know the life style of a gangbanger, it costs." He said, looking at Marybeth and Marianne.

"Your brother?" she asked, just assuming.

"Sister." He said solemnly "Drive by shooting, you know how it goes?"

She shook her head no; he laughed and said "Good." She just looked at him, waiting for him to say something else. It was silent for a few minutes. He could feel the presence of her eyes on his shoulders.

"Say something" he said finally "I can't take it"

She smiled and put her hand on his arm "What happened to her?"

"She's fine, well not according to her," he said, pausing "Paralyzed her, and now she lives with my mom, I haven't talked to her since."

"That's awful." Chrys said

"I know, okay" he snapped sitting up, as he had been leaning back with her "I didn't mean for it to happen."

"No, Kal, that's not what I meant" she said grabbing his hand "I meant that you haven't talked to her."

He sighed, his hand was shaking, she pulled him over and put her arm around his shoulder.

"I'm sorry" they said at the same time, Chrys smiled and put her hand on his back.

"Chrys," he asked, "why are my hands shaking?"

"I don't know," she said, taking them in hers, "but it's all right."

"You know, the last thing I said to her was 'eh, you'll get over it, didn't kill ya. Seem pretty lucky to me'. I hate myself for that."

Chrys rubbed her hand up and down his back; Kalvin took everything he had to just keep composed.

"You shouldn't, Kalvin, you've been out of the game for how many years?" Chrys asked, she knew how long he'd been out she just wanted him to say it.

"Two, almost" he said softly.

"Right and Kalvin that guy was a different person, a hurting and scared person. But, Kalvin you don't have to be scared anymore." She told him, hugging his chest "It's all okay, now. You can always make up with your sister it's never too late. *Never.*"

"Yes, it is, we're stuck here and- and..."

"No, no, no Kal we'll get home okay? And then I'll take you to your sister, okay?" she told him rubbing her hands up and down his arms.

He nodded and went over to his spot, to sleep. But, he got back up and walked back over to Chrys. He squatted down in front of her, wrapped his arms around her shoulders and kissed the back of her neck. Even though he'd kissed her head like that before it made goose bumps crawl up and down her arm.

He went back over to his spot and went to sleep then. She watched him for a minute, as he slept, before going to sleep herself.

The next day they set off to their separate chores. Chrys went to look for water, the twins went for wood and reeds and stuff, they guys went to the mud hole.

"Ready?" Frank asked as they dug through the dried mud to get to the jeep, again.

"For what?" Kalvin asked, by his guess it was only five am, the sun hadn't even come up yet

"Never mind" Frank mumbled

"Tell me" Kalvin protested, now waist deep in mud

"Well, dude it's been like fricken a year, dude just ask her out." Frank said harshly

Kalvin just stared at him for a minute "Do you really think someone like her would want to date someone like *me*? Dude, you're out of your fricken mind!"

"Are you blind!?" Frank said loudly "the girls in deep with you man! I'd bet she'd say yes faster than you'd get the question out."

"Yeah, right!" Kalvin laughed "She's rich, beautiful, kind, caring! Why would she go for a no good gangbangin' loser?"

"You tell me what she would do if she heard you say that?" Frank asked

"She'd probably slap me" Kalvin told him hauling a box to land

"Right and she'd tell you 'Kalvin, that's not true. You've made mistakes, who hasn't? But, you're a good person; you've done something with your life' Am I right?"

"Dude, she's actually said that!" Kalvin said, not really sure what to think

"That's what I get for having a girl as a best friend. The play-by-play." Frank laughed handing Kalvin another box.

"How many do we have left?" Kalvin asked

"Um," Frank said feeling around "I think that's it"

"Awesome, well I guess we'd better start cleaning em" Kalvin said looking at the sky; he'd guessed it'd been about three hours. They'd work right up until it got dark.

"Let's start with the dried ones in the cave" Frank said

They ran back to the cave grabbed the dried bags and brought them back down. The things in the bags came out relatively clean. Only one or two things got some mud on it. They scraped the mud off with their hands and with flat rocks. They decided that they could spare two bottles of water to clean them off better with. They decided to bring them back up to the cave and then try to figure out how to get the jeep out.

"We could tie, like vines to it and pull it out, or something." Kalvin suggested.

"I don't think the two of us, two eleven year old twins, and a girl with leukemia can pull it out" Frank said smiling, he hoped Kal wouldn't take it the wrong way. It took a few seconds, but he cracked a smile.

"I don't know, I guess we'll just have to wait and see. Is it noon yet?" Kalvin asked

"I don't know but, I'm gonna start cleaning them now." Frank said hopping up and walking back down and over to the bags.

"Okay" Kalvin said following, they found most of the bags were dry or mostly dry. It got hot during the day, in where-ever-land. They scraped what they could off and wiped it down with the water. They tried to save as much water as they could. They lugged all the luggage back up to the cave, and as they finally sat down to rest a sudden wave of dizziness rushed over Kalvin. They hadn't eaten in days, and he knew they couldn't go much longer. So he decided since they finished early they should look for food, any kind of food. Or some method of making fire so they could cook.

"We need weapons." Frank said after Kalvin told him of his plan.

"Okay well we could tie like rocks to a long stick and use it like spears people survived on those for hundreds of years. And since I can't manufacture a gun or pull one out of my ass it'll have to do." Kalvin smiled

"Oh yeah" Frank smiled "I'll get the sticks you get the rocks and whatever to fasten them with, k?"

"K" Kalvin said and they were off again...

****

"Where are we?" Marybeth whined, "I don't even remember what we're supposed to be doing anymore"

"We're supposed to be gathering supplies for our hut-thing." Marianne told her

"Right well here the tree they picked...*ohmigod*!" Marybeth nearly yelled

"What?!" Marianne asked startled

"Look at that, we're really close to a mountain!" Marybeth squealed

"Chrys could be close; she's looking for water, should we go get her?" Marianne asked

"No, she'd be mad that we didn't do our job right"

"True, true. Okay Chrys said we need reeds or like stalks and um, like flexible wood and straw maybe. Stuff like that"

"Okay well stalks could be near the ocean and flexible wood, would too. So let's go there."

"Okay."

They walked for about twenty minutes and all they saw was hills and trees. They were starting to get worried; they thought they might be heading inland instead of outland. But they decided to walk for a couple more minutes, and just before they decided to turn back, a gust of wind blew the smell of the ocean to them.

"Yay!" they squealed and using what could be the last of their energy ran to the ocean. They threw themselves down in the sand and let the ocean water splash over them. After a few minutes, Marianne got up, wiped the sand off her and started to look for the reeds.

"Come on, Beth!" she called to her "I think I see some"

21

Marybeth ran to catch up to her.

"Wait" she yelled and Marianne stopped to wait for her "What did you see?"

"Some reeds" Marianne answered pointing to a spot about five yards up the beach. "Let's go"

"Okay" Marybeth said and they ran the whole way to the reeds. When they got there, there was a whole patch of reeds with some wired looking stalk things in them. They decided to take as much as they could carry of both the reeds and the other things and put them in front of their path the one they came out. But that took too long, carrying them back and forth and they had already wasted a lot of time playing in the ocean.

"This isn't working Anne," Marybeth said, "We need to find a better way to get them there"

"Well we could just make a big pile of all that we need and take them load for load that way" Marianne suggested "Or we could go see if the guys are done and ask them to help us."

"Um, we should try the first one and if it doesn't work we'll ask them. It would waste a lot of time to go get them now, right?" Marybeth said looking around for something stronger than the reeds. They wouldn't hold up a fort if there were to be bad weather.

"Right, what are you looking for?" Marianne asked

"Oh, um just something stronger for the outside"

"Oh, okay well let's get this back there now" Marianne said "Then we can find something"

"Okay" Marybeth said and they started to pick up as much as they could carry then and drag it back to the tree. It took them a good hour to bring it all there and at that, they saw the guys coming through the woods.

"Hey need help?" Kalvin asked and breathlessly they agreed, so the four of them took the rest back to the cave.

"Have you guys seen any like harder things to build with?" Marianne asked

"No, but we can look" Frank said

"Hey, how do you think Chrys is doin?" Kalvin whispered to Frank as they walked

****

Chrys walked alone in the forest for the some odd amount of time. The whole time she just thought. She thought about her illness and her parents and her friends but mostly she thought of Kalvin. She thought of everything he meant to her and everything he had done for her. She thought of everything she'd done for him but no matter what she thought of nothing compared to what she had done to him. She got him stranded on an island, with no food or water and yet he remained loyal to her. Why, she didn't know. She thought of asking him, but didn't know how. And she cried, she cried for him and for her. She cried for her sisters and Frank. She cried for the loss of everything they left behind and she cried for the prospects of any of them getting off this island. And she cried for the fact that for the first time she realized no matter how much she lived life to the fullest she'll never be able to make up for what eventually her disease is going to take from her. She'd always put on a smile and had a positive attitude almost to the point of naivety, but, she wasn't naïve she was scared. But, now as she walked alone in the woods of an island she realized what she'd hidden for years, slowly if not surly she was dying. That somewhat that scared her and somewhat it didn't. She knew that whatever she did in her last days had to be great, but everything she could think of would be waiting for her at the cave when she found her way back. She smiled at that thought; it took being stranded on a deserted island for to finally see. She'd been searching for all these years since she got sick, when she already had everything right in front of her. She wiped her eyes and realized she'd walked right to the base of a mountain; she looked all around and thought perhaps- just maybe there was a ledge. And maybe that ledge was a waterfall. She smiled and speed walked back to the cave, finding no one there she walked towards their tree and back to the cave when she found the group walking there with the last load.

"Hey!" she waved, "Guess what. I think I found a waterfall. Well I walked to a mountain, there looked like there could be a ridge on the other side, and I was thinking that there could be waterfall. It's worth a shot isn't it?"

23

"Yeah, so tonight we should make a fire and eat, cause I'm starved and start out tomorrow morning. What do you think?"

"I think we should find that waterfall and go swimming" Marybeth said "or take showers cause y'all stink!"

"Oh really and you think you smell like roses?" Marianne asked laughing

"Okay, well let's see if we brought a lighter or something to start a fire with" Chrys said

"I think we brought a lighter but I don't know how long it will last" Kalvin told her

"Well let's cross that bridge when we get there" Chrys said softly and he nodded

"Hey! Hey come here" Marianne called and they ran to her

"Look, it's flint I think" Frank said

"Break some off" Chrys said to Kalvin, positive he could break small layer of rock on the ground easily. He picked up a rock and smashed on the flint until some broke off. They picked it up and walked back to the cave gather wood along the way. They started a fire in the middle of the floor and cooked up some eggs, trying to be easy on their stomachs, but, the dizziness went away and they felt better, stronger for the next day's journey.

****

"*That mountain* we have to climb *that* mountain?" Marybeth said

"Yes, there might be food and water over there, Beth" Marianne said quietly "Sometimes you have to think of more than yourself"

Marybeth shot her a death look but after years of that Marianne just ignored it and went on

"Chrys has to climb that mountain, too." Marianne told her, shooting her own look

"Oh, yeah Chrys, Chrys, Chrys. It's not all about her!" Marybeth whined

"Beth!" Marianne snapped, "She could be dying!"

"No, she's not! Mary, she's not!" Beth told her

"Chrys has to say that she's our big sister, she has to, but, she could be dying!"

"Guys, she's not dying" Kal said his face white like it did every time her death was mentioned.

"I'm not climbing back and forth to store and get stuff." Marybeth moaned

"You wouldn't anyway" Marianne protested, "We've got to do what we've got to do to survive"

"Guys" Chrys coughed, she was still very weak, even more so after walking the whole day before "We need to get going"

"Okay" they mumbled

Kalvin stood watching her frail body shake as she coughed Frank elbowed him.

"Uh-mh" he cleared his throat "Chrys, Chrys do-do you need my- I mean if you need any- um"

She smiled and put her hand on his shoulder, and said:

"Thanks."

He smiled unsure of what to do; he knew she wouldn't be able to make it on her own. She just moved wearily toward the mountain. Slowly looking up at it.

"Kal," she said softly "I won't make it up"

He smiled "That's fine," he pushed her hair out of her face.

Up ahead, Marianne turned to Frank then "Does he love her?"

Frank shrugged and moved on, but he looked back and said one thing "Does it matter?"

Marianne shook her head and looked at them "Nope, she's dying isn't she?" tears welling up in her eyes.

"Marianne, she'd kill me for saying so but in all probability; yes." he said solemnly.

"Why does God take the innocent?" Marianne asked

Frank smiled and said, "To punish the guilty"

"Like who?" she asked her eyes searching the ground for an answer "Me, Beth? You?"

"No" he shook his head and gestured to Kalvin who was smiling and wrapping his blanket around Chrys "*Him*"

Marianne stared at Kalvin trying to ask but the words never formed at her lips. Marybeth's face fumed, she had been listening silently from a short distance. She ran back to Kalvin.

"What did you do?! Why?! You're killing her!!" she screamed and punched his chest over and over.

Kalvin, who was a very big man just stood there and let her hit him. Even as she screamed in hysteria, he knew what Frank had told them and he knew what she meant. In his mind, it was about time someone called him out on it, but what could he do Chrys didn't know everything that had happened. Frank ran over and held her back Chrys just stared speechless.

Eventually she just uttered the words "Beth, what?"

"Him-him- Frank said-h-him!" she panted pointing at him accusingly

"No," Marianne spoke up "he said God takes the innocent to punish the guilty, like Kalvin."

Chrys turned to Frank and shook her head.

"Something's," she said harshly, not knowing what Frank knew and what he really meant, "just need to remain unsaid" and walked away

She had to stop to catch her breath and could hear Frank and Kalvin screaming at each other. Softer at first, then louder and louder.

"What the hell are you doing telling them she's dying?"

"That's not what I said!" Frank protested

"You didn't not say it!"

"Quit pretending Kalvin! Get your head out of the freaking clouds!" Frank told him lowering his voice, but Chrys cold still hear "She is" Before Chrys could even think Kalvin wailed him; Frank stumbled and fell to the ground. He got up screaming

"Stop hiding what you are, Kalvin! Quit lying to her! Why didn't you tell her? You're disgusting!"

"Stop it!" Chrys yelled, turning around, tears pouring from her eyes.

Kalvin just closed his mouth and reached his hand out, not really reaching her.

She took his hand and wrapped hers around it, milky white she seemed so surreal. He felt almost like if he reached out he would pass right through her.

"I'm sick, yes. But, I'm not dying. So please stop saying that I am" she was looking at Frank then "and everybody, just stop it okay, I don't think talking about it is gonna make it better."

"Okay? Frank I love you you're my best friend but you should learn to keep your mouth shut!" she said looking him straight in the eyes, in all the time she'd been sick she'd trusted what he'd told her, but now she didn't even care if he was right.

She stood firmly and waited as they walked ahead. Eventually she started walking again, putting distance between her and Frank, she was pissed. She had Kal's hand as they walked and he rubbed his other hand up and down her back.

"I-I need to tell you something." he told her in a hushed tone

"You don't have to." she whispered

"I do though" he told her as she leaned her head in on his chest "I-I've done some bad things in my time. I've stolen and-and hurt some people."

"You did what you had to" she told him with sympathetic eyes "I may never fully understand but I'm okay with it."

"But I-I nearly killed someone." he whispered

"I understand," she told him even though she didn't. Inside her stomach flipped, she knew he'd done some bad things but not murder. Outside she just kept her calm. "It's okay. Things happen; the point is you've done some bad things, that doesn't make you a bad person." She had the fullest confidence in him that whatever he did he had to do it. There had to be no other way.

"I-I he-he tried to kill me I-I didn't have a choice." he stammered not really looking at her or anyone

"You don't have to tell me." she whispered, he couldn't hear it but in her voice there was a slight glimmer of hope that he wouldn't tell her. She didn't want to know, she really just wanted him to stop talking but then again she knew she should know. That she needed to.

He nodded and went on "It was the day I met you, when you were getting your cousin or whatever out of jail. You-you were what? Fifteen. I was walking down the street and there was this guy, I-I didn't know him but he was in the Vista gang, I was in the Downtown Viper's. You know that, though. I just walked by, and he came out with a gun, so I pulled mine and shot. I didn't even think about it. I ran and ran, and then I literally ran into you. I was covered in blood and you made me go to the hospital."

****

Chrys was walking down the street lecturing her cousin about how she's gonna kill him if he ever does that again. When Kalvin came running out of the alley, looked back and slammed into her

"S-sorry." he said helping her up, once she smiled and said she was fine he was on his way again

"Wait! Are you hurt, you're covered in blood?"

"No, I'm fine" he said pulling away from her grip, which she just now noticed was on his arm

"Sorry, but, I think you should go to the hospital" she said "You don't look so good"

"You don't look so hot yourself" he mumbled

"I don't have to" she said calmly "I have leukemia"

He just didn't say anything then. She stood there smiling.

Eventually, he said "Maybe I should go to the hospital" she nodded and laughed

"Apology accepted" she told him as they walked to the hospital. That was how she knew he wasn't just another gangbanger. A gangbanger would've left, would've been worse.

****

Chrys smiled at the memory "I remember that, but why didn't you get in trouble?"

"Gangbangers never rat on each other" he told her squeezing her hand even tighter

"Oh" she said simply "I'm sorry"

"Why?" he asked

"That you had to live that way" she told him "It's not true you know, God doesn't always take the innocent. He takes the privileged so they can know what it's like to not have anything. That's why" she said looking at her sisters "it was them or me. And I'm glad it's me."

"I'm not" he told her and she laughed and coughed simultaneously

"Hey look" he said "We're like a fourth of the way up"

She smiled and laughed.

"Anytime you need help just-just ask." he whispered as she heaved for breath

She gave him thumbs up and they went on. They climbed on for hours before she had to give up completely, she'd been struggling to keep going for some time.

"Kal- Kal" she heaved heavily "I-I can't, I can't"

"That's okay" he told her "I'll carry you"

29

She looked at him and smiled, before her knees buckled under her. She looked up with big, dark eyes and laughed.

"What?" he asked and she shook her head and reached her arms up

He laughed now and bent over, his back facing her. She climbed on, holding lightly. She put her hands on his chest and whispered in his ear "I can feel your heart beat"

He looked back at her as the sun set and kissed her cheek, then in a soft voice whispered "So can I"

Her face turned flush, and for the first time in a long time, she felt alive. And as the stars over head shined and moon glinted in her eyes, they reached the top of the mountain.

"Look-look" Chrys shouted from Kalvins back "I was right! A ledge!"

He looked back at her and smiled.

"I'm not heavy am I?" she asked, her eyes wide with excitement

"Never" he said, and she wasn't she hadn't eaten for days except for yesterday and her medication made her loose more weight, and she wouldn't have been heavy to begin with. Marianne was carrying that currently, her medicine, Frank carried it for most of the way.

"*Ohmigod*!" Marybeth squealed "a waterfall!"

"Water?" Chrys asked, she'd only seen the cliff and wondered if there were any trees near it, she still wasn't thinking completely clear "I want some water, you should have some water, too."

"Me too" Marybeth whined as she ran toward it bending over and scooping the water into her mouth, the rest followed and Kalvin helped Chrys drink

Marybeth watched with disgust "You know you could think about *him*, once"

"She did," he snapped, "I forced her to let me help her"

"You didn't force her to let you carry her up the mountain"

"There was no other way!" he snapped at her, he was furious and it showed in his face. She was his everything even if she didn't know it and when that was attacked, he flipped a switch and was the Kalvin the streets had known. Chrys knew better than to think that though, she knew he was protecting her. Because he thought, she needed it and she wasn't going to argue.

"There had to be! There's always another way, ever since she got sick all you've done is take care of her! She never thinks of anyone but herself anymore! I'm so sick of it being all about her! If it weren't for her we wouldn't be here right now, we'd be home safe and happy. But, no, Chrys had to take us here because Chrys wanted to because it's all about her!" she screamed at him, Marianne stood shocked, Chrys just stared at them and Frank, of course, had to get involved.

"Hey! Hey!! Hey!!!" he screamed, "Stop it! First off, Marybeth shut the hell up! You don't know shit about what you're talking about! And Kal, chill out man! She's eleven, lay off."

Kalvin walked off, swearing under his breath. Marybeth went to speak up but Chrys beat her to it.

"Marybeth" Chrys spoke up "I am extremely upset with you right now-no, no, I'm pissed! What-what we're you thinking? I can answer that, you weren't! You have to get over yourself, or we'll never make it here- you won't!"

"And second, my whole life has been about the two of you and have I ever complained, no. So I got sick and wanted to do something for myself finally, so what! I'm sorry we're lost, I'm sorry that we have to live here. But, can you please think of someone else every now and then! And you know what, you will be sorry when I'm gone." She got up and followed Kalvin, weak kneed, tripping and stumbling along the way.

"Kal! Kal wait!" she called and he stopped and turned around

"I'm sorry" he told her "I know she only a kid but-"

"No, I'm sorry. I'm sorry she's being such a brat and I'm sorry she's right. I've been just relying on you and I'm not sure I've ever even thanked you for helping me all these years. But, Kalvin you have to know something-"

He stopped her then; he took her face in his hands and kissed her. She looked up at him and smiled.

"K-Kalvin" she said

"I-I ...I'm sorry" he said quickly

"No, don't be. That's exactly what I wanted to say but- but couldn't" She said wrapping her arms around his neck "Thank you for everything you've done for me. And Kal I'm not gonna die, I'm not going anywhere"

"You're not allowed to" he told her

"Really?" she asked smiling her face inches from his

"Really, because I have an important question for you" he said as a gentle rained beat down on them

She smiled and teased, "I hope it's a good one."

"Well I hope it is too." He said whispering in her ear "Chrys would- will you"

She nodded smiling and he squeezed her close. Her frail body fitting perfectly in his arms.

"We should get back" he said and she nodded, she took his hand and they walked back. They sat down near the waterfall and this time he drank the water. She sat there and watched him. Eventually they tried to estimate how far they were from the cave and the tree.

And trying to fill the awkward silence they decided to go look for a closer tree the next day. And they slept, woke, and walked. They walked to a tree and decided that this was going to be theirs. On top of the mountain and near the waterfall. They sent Frank and Kalvin to retrieve the building materials and they were back in a matter of hours to find the girls had fastened together a makeshift sled type thing. They wove together some smaller reeds they found near the waterfall.

"Hey" Chrys said looking up "Is that all of it?"

"Yeah" Kalvin said

"Wow! Seriously you must be carrying like 150 pounds," Chrys said helping to unload him "Well I suppose we should start now"

They fastened ropes to the tree and lifted each other up, except for the twins who stayed on the ground. The twins dragged the material to the new tree and helped rip small branches and pile them for kindling. Chrys and the boys found the branches with the most level of a surface. They laid the strongest flattest reeds down and fastened them with a rope they got off the jeep. They hoisted the twins up using the lowest branches they had, after they ripped the kindling off the tree, and the the other rope the twins had gotten. At that time, the first day of work was over. After that, they wove inner walls together, using a method Chrys had basically invented when they were making the sled type thing. They took mud from the bottom of the waterfall, which they had sent the twins to the bottom of. It was about thirty feet high by their guess, with a lake below it, and small streams running from it. They packed the mud into the cracks, and spread it into the floor. Subsequently the second day was over. Next, they took the thicker reeds and built and outer wall. They wove tighter a roof with thick and thin boards. They took the clay and the reeds and wove fasteners around the tree and repeat for a connecting room. They built clay steps coming down from the tree, but those fell apart causing Kalvin to tumble to the ground. Other than a few scrapes and bruises, he was fine, however. They decided that they needed to keep Chrys up there to get the stuff and see if they needed to build another room on it because so far they only made two. They took the make shift sled and hauled their things up with it. They cut the rope, which was approximately 20 feet long, in half. Tying one half of the rope that they had used to hoist each other up, around the stuff and tying the other end in a loop, which they used to pull it up. Presently the third day of labor was over. Then they got them up as far as they could on the tree by climbing, handed Chrys the things and she arranged them in the rooms. One room for the boys and one for the girls. She called down:

"We need another storage room!"

"Okay" Kalvin called and they built one. Wove the walls, built the floors, dried clay, and stuck them together with it. She arranged everything and pulled her sisters up. They managed to climb the branches just as it started to rain on the fourth day of their work.

"Chrys" Kalvin said, "Can we make a fire?"

"I can try," she said, "I left a little room in the floor for it, see?"

There was a little hole in the floor, surrounded by clay so the house wouldn't burn down. There was clay for two or three inches on the top along the floor and the bottom and sides were entirely clay. They got some kindling from the corner of the room. There was the girls' room then the storage/ living room/ kitchen and then the boys' room. She cooked up some of their food and she lay down on the floor near Kalvin and slept. Kalvin carried her to her room, laid her down on the makeshift bed, and covered her up.

"Kal" she whispered as he was leaving

"Yeah?" he asked

"Come here" she said motioning for him to come over to her

He did and she just wrapped her arms around his torso and he sat near her, hugging her shoulders. She laid her head on his chest. They just sat there for a minute before he said anything.

"Chrys what's wrong?" he asked and she looked up at him

"I don't know," she said, "I just wanted to be near you"

"That's totally okay with me." he told her the warm night air seeping in.

She laughed and said "Good" as Frank walked in

"Um, Kal" Frank said walking in "Never mind"

"No come here!" Chrys called and he walked over and bent down "Guess what?"

"What?" he asked

"I don't know" she laughed, "You always go for that!"

"Chrys did you take your medicine?" Frank asked

"Yes, I'm just happy" she said laughing; "Can't a girl have a little fun? I mean being stranded on an island can't be so gloomy all the time, it's gonna get very dispiriting and dreary."

"I guess, anyway we need to get some like place to store water, just in case something happens." Frank suggested

"Okay, first thing tomorrow" Chrys said walking back out into the living room with the girls.

"So, let's play a game, like they used to in the olden days" Chrys said "Sit in a circle. Everybody close their eyes and hold out their dominate hand."

"Okay"

"Now everybody tap someone's hand but don't make it easy. Okay? Ready? On the count of three open your eyes, 1, 2, 3!"

"Going from left to right Marybeth you start" she said "Youngest first"

"Okay um, I guess now right?" she asked and Chrys nodded "Okay, I don't know, Frank?" she guessed and he nodded no.

"Okay" my turn Marianne said "Um, Chrys?"

"Nope! My turn! Um, Bethy?" she said looking all around her

"Yes! How did you know?" she asked loudly, she had a way of being loud and boisterous

"Don't know" Chrys said softly

"Okay, my turn" Frank said "Um, Kal?"

"Naw" he said "Okay...Marianne?" he asked

"Yeah, how did you get that?" she asked

"You were the only one left," he said and when she gave him a puzzled look, he went on "I choose Marybeth. Marybeth chose Chrys, and Chrys had to choose Frank, me, or you then. Frank had to choose either you or me. So that leaves you, I guess"

The twins stared at him and he shrugged. Chrys smiled, she knew he was smarter than he let on. His whole he'd been the bad boy, the tough guy. Being smart would ruin that. But, to Chrys he was perfect in all his imperfections.

****

"Come on girls, we need to get a move on it!" Kalvin called from the ground below the hut

"Coming!" Chrys called hopping down to the first branch, as she made her way down she said "You guys should find a good place to store things that's closer than the cave, plus we need a place to keep perishables, cause soaking them in water isn't gonna work for much longer and we need the meat. Plus I'm gonna stay here and do laundry and maybe make some storage baskets, but, you guys should take the girls with you so they have something to do. Plus we need to make more weapons for hunting, if we have any anyways."

"Okay," Kalvin said helping her down from the last branch, it's about a three foot drop.

"I'm good, help the girls down" she told him

"Okay" he said helping them down as Chrys began to gather her things

"Where are you guys going so I know where to go?" she asked, she either seemed anxious or hyper

"Wait we need to decide whose doing what" Kalvin said

"Okay, well I'm gonna do laundry and make baskets but that shouldn't take too awfully long so I can also do something else"

"Um, okay how bout you find a place to store the perishables" Marianne suggested

"Perfect!" she said "and you girls will go with the guys and do whatever they say"

"Ugh!" Marybeth whined but before it went any further, Frank spoke

"I'll make weapons and Kal can look for a place to store thing. I'll take one kid you take the other." he said and they departed.

Chrys stayed there and for four or so hours, she made baskets and brought them up to the hut filled them and threw down clothes. She climbed down to the bottom of the waterfall taking the clothes with her. She scrubbed the clothes against a rock then rinsed them in the side waterfall. The side waterfall is a small waterfall that flows down off the rocks next to the waterfall; it comes from one of the many streams flowing into the waterfall that just happened to be cut off by rocks. It juts off where the rocks stick out further than the big waterfall. After she laid them on a tree-branch to dry and wove a few baskets, carried them back up and sorted what they need with what they can store away. About half way down she began to slip. Her foot searched and searched for a place to sneak in and save herself. Against her better judgment, she looked down and her feet slipped again at the glaring drop. Her strength was depleted; it took all she had just to hold on. Slowly she shifted her weight closer and closer to an over lying branch. In a leap of faith and strength, she jumped a good foot, grabbed onto a low hanging branch, and twisted around. She shoved her feet into the ground and pulled herself up, all the while feeling the branch struggle to hold her. She reached an area where the solid incline gives way to the flat rock and pulled herself up to safety. As she stood and slowly steadied herself, she noticed a small cavern -like thing behind the big waterfall. She inched her way closer to get a better look. As climbed slowly over the small waterfall until she was on a ledge near the waterfall, she decided to try to construct a bridge. She knew she would need planks, but she couldn't make them herself. She also knew most likely, it would only hold her and the twins. She grabbed the strongest vines and branches she could and hacked them off with a stone, which she splintered on a bigger stone. She wove them together as best she could using mud from the bottom of the river to plaster her weaving together. Once she was finished, she climbed back up to the place where she saw the cave. She took some mudplaster she carried in her shirt and globbed it onto the stone and around the end of her bridge. She sat on them until they hardened then she yanked and pulled with all her might and whatever cracks and broke off she redid. Once she was done she made another, and then another, but the third one she made was for the hut, so she laid the other two on the rock to dry. Taking the third, she climbed back up the waterfall, taking a clump of mudplaster in her shirt. She climbed up the tree and plastered the ladder on floor of the doorway. Once she was done she hauled down the perishable foods and then down the waterfall, too.

****

"Keeping up?" Kal asked Marianne

"Yup, I'm coming, but, what are we supposed to do again?" she asked running to keep up with his large strides

"Looking for storage." He told her shoving the roughage out of their way

"We should go a different way; we've gone too far to make it easy to get to."

"No I think we should just go a little further, um, just around that corner." he said pointing to a bend

"Fine." she said sighing, "You know, this place is sooo boring."

"Yeah." he said quickly

"You're kinda scary, do you know that?" she asked quietly

"I've heard." he said

"Oh" she said softly, as they came upon a small indentation in the rocky mountain.

"Here, we can just dig some out and construct a door somehow, I guess" he said pulling away at some loose and crumbling rock. "Help me"

"Okay," she said pushing the rocks; he threw out of the way. They dug at the top with a large stone trying to break more away. The indentation was about three feet deep and they needed it about six feet, but there was about a foot and a half of loose rubble in the way. Once they dug the rubble out the sun was high in the sky and very hot, and they just hit hard rock. It was at this point that Kalvin really began to wonder why this was happening to them. For the first time as they sat there, hiding from the heat he really let himself think about where they were and what they were up against. At first, it was pure adrenaline and the need to survive, but, now they were okay for a while and he could think. Why? Why, was this happening, why them, why now, why *ever*? Why is Chrys sick? Why can't he stop thinking about the streets and his old life? He looked over at the young girl sitting there, knowing that if she were to get sick from the heat he would help her, knowing he wouldn't let her die. But, did he know that, could he really tell himself that in his normal state of mind he would have done anything he'd done in the last weeks? He didn't and that scared him, he needed to know that he wasn't using Chrys. He knew how he thought he felt, but, never, he never knew how he really felt. Not now and not in the past year. Eventually he just got up and started smashing rocks against the indentation. Telling Marianne to sit down. He smashed with anger and she smashed with fear. To let everything out he smashed with everything he had. At length, it ended up loosening the rocks enough to make a big enough space for their things. He sent Marianne back through the woods to get the things he was exhausted. He knew it wasn't fair to make her do it but he just couldn't move. His body just lay limp under the afternoon sun. Marianne came back with Chrys in tow and the whole lot of extra things. They shoved the things in there and Chrys started to weave a reed and tall grass door, and eventually let Marianne finish it.

"Hey, are you okay?" Chrys asked Kalvin as he lay in the sun

She felt his head and it was way too hot, she ran back to the hut as fast as her sick body would let her, lugging water in a jug they'd brought she poured it over him and gave him some to drink. She laid his head in her lap as Marianne wove a door.

"I'm sorry I can't take better care of you. Considering that's what you've been doing for me since I met you." She said sopping the end of her shirt and rubbing it on his head.

"No, you've been fine" he said closing his eyes as she lay her hands on his chest

She didn't know the symptoms of heat stroke but she was very worried as he began to cough and shake. As he shook more and more violently Chrys prayed that Marybeth and Frank came back soon.

****

"Marybeth! You need to keep up!" Frank ordered as they walked "It's going to get dark soon and we haven't even come close to finding anything to make weapons out of."

"I don't see why we need them." she whined

"Well, we need to eat, and defend ourselves in case there are animals on this island."

"Fine" she said yanking some bamboo-looking things out of the ground, "We have the bottoms"

Frank took it from her and said, "No, we have sugar"

"Sugar?" she asked

39

"Yeah look, it's a sugar cane" he showed her the sugar just below the top of the cane

"Awesome!" she said pulling four more out and setting them aside "Can we come back for them?"

"Yea" he said and they pulled out some reeds to use as sticks for weapons, whatever weapons they did have were gone or forgotten.

Frank broke rocks on other rocks and tried to shape them into spears but they ended up looking more like squished tomahawks. So he wrapped the tops in his shirt and again tried to make spears with better luck this time, wrapping those in his shirt and grabbing the bottom half they headed back. Marybeth grabbing the sugar canes on the way, as they walked they stumbled upon Chrys and Kalvin, Marianne had been sent back to the hut as it was getting dark. The reed door Marianne had woven had been fastened in placed on the cave door.

"What happened?" he asked sitting down next to the crying Chrys

"He-he I don't know it was hot out and he couldn't get up. I-I don't know what to do, he started shaking and coughing and now he can't breathe. Please help him Frank, please. I-I know you don't like him but-"

"Chrys, move." he said and she slid out from under him

"Thank you" she whispered and he nodded towards Marybeth, who watched as Kalvin convulsed and trembled on the ground.

"Go back to the hut, take the stuff and have your sister fix dinner, okay?" she said as Marybeth stared

"Is he-" she started to ask

"Just go it'll be fine" she told her kissing the top of her head. Marybeth took the thing and ran back to the hut.

****

"Anne, Anne?" she called as she stood at the bottom of the rope ladder "Help me bring these things up"

Marianne helped bring the things up and then she fixed a small dinner and wrapped some in a shirt, "One of us needs to take this to them"

"I can't go back there" Marybeth stared at the floor "He-he was"

"I'll go" Marianne said climbing down and running to Chrys, she wasn't too fond of the dark and Marybeth knew that but even she was past her antics. She was truly shocked and a little traumatized.

"Here, it's food" Marianne said holding the food out to Chrys, she took it and set it aside

"Go back" she ordered and Marianne ran back and as fast as she could she climbed up the rope ladder.

"Was he still?-" Marybeth asked not able to say it and Marianne nodded. At that point, Beth was sitting on the ground and Marianne just wrapped her arms around her sister and sat there.

****

"Frank, Frank is he gonna be okay?" Chrys asked looking at him as if he could do something about it

"I don't know" Frank said struggling to hold Kalvins body down

After a few more minutes they thought it was over, the convulsing subsided, the coughing stopped and he just laid there. But, after a minute, it became obvious that he wasn't breathing any more.

"Kalvin? Kalvin?! Kalvin, wake up!!!" Chrys screamed and the girls heard her from the hut

Frank just flipped around, straddled his chest, and performed CPR to the best of his knowledge. After a minute Kalvin coughed again and Chrys could breathe once more. He opened his eyes slowly and sat up. His shirt was ripped and tattered in the back from thrashing around on the ground. He was disoriented and it took a moment for the world to stop spinning around him. His heart was pounding when he realized it was dark and he didn't know where Chrys was.

"Chrys? Chrys! Chrys!!" he yelled his voice swelling with every frightened yell

"I'm here, I'm right here." she said crawling over toward him taking him in her arms, he shook in the night air.

"You should go in Chrys, the air isn't good for you." Frank said placing a hand on her shoulder.

"But-" she started and he shook his head. She gave him a warning look, he nodded, and she left.

"Kalvin" he started helping him up

"I know it was dumb," Kalvin said "I should've been more careful. I just wasn't helping enough, I don't know."

"Kalvin, you've done more for her in the two years- or so- that you've known her than I have in the ten that I've known her." Frank told him grabbing Kalvins arm as he swayed

"Look, kid, you know what I've done and she doesn't. Do-do you think I could do it again?" he asked as they slowly walked

"Do you love her?" Frank asked

Kalvin was silent for a second before he said "Yea, yes. Yes."

"Then no I don't think you could, not if you love her enough" Frank said, "she's like my sister and she's always trusted what I say except for when it comes to you. When it's you it doesn't even matter if I told her everything you'd done she wouldn't care. Just tell me something, okay?"

"What?" Kalvin asked

"That even if she gets really sick you'll never leave her, don't hurt her. She can't take anymore hurt." He told Kalvin as they approached the hut

"You've never hurt her though." Kalvin told him

"As far as you two know." Frank told him "I might not have come from downtown but that doesn't make me a saint."

"I don't understand" Kalvin said as Frank helped him climb up the ladder, his arms were shaking even under the little bit of strain

"She likes the people everyone else has given up on" he told him as they reached the top, "I wasn't good, but not as bad as you. I was a dropout druggie with no care for who I hurt. But, I made a promise and I broke it."

"I thought you met when you were like 7?"

"We did, but just because I met her didn't mean I liked her. Our parents were business associates, and we were forced to be together a lot, but until I was like 13-14 we didn't speak more than 'hi'. That's about the time I got sick of being forced to miss parties, and whatever so I snuck out you know that kinda stuff. But when I hit 15, I found drugs and booze. And then she found me. So I promised by my 16th birthday I would be off of the drugs-"

"Wait isn't that the year I met her?"

"Yea, a lot happened that year, I stopped because she got sick, but she thought I stopped before that. Anyway, I guess the whole point of me telling you this was to tell you why I'm so hard on your past, because I know how easily she'll believe you're a good person even if you go back to doing what you did."

"I swear I'm out, I'm done." Kalvin said hands up, "I'll never leave."

"Good, then we're cool?" Frank asked

"We're cool." Kalvin said, and they hugged it out, in the way, Chrys always said wasn't hugging. it was high-fiving then smacking each other's back.

They walked into the hut and Chrys stood up, she had been sitting with Marybeth and Marianne.

"Go to bed girls" she said and they ran into the other room

"I'll be in the other room." Kal said walking away

"But-" Chrys said turning to stop him, but he just looked at Frank and back at her.

Chrys turned to Frank who stood in the doorway. She walked over and threw her arms around his neck. He stood surprised for a minute, she had been really

43

disconnected since she and Kalvin became more serious. Eventually he brought his hands up to hug her back. Kalvin, who watched from the doorway, laughed to himself. Chrys let Frank go from her grasp, but she pulled him over around the fire pit.

"Frank, I need to tell you something- something I should've said a long time ago and a whole lot more than I do." She told him sitting next to him the way a little sister sits next to her brother when she's scared or shy.

"Wait- Chrys I need to tell you something, too" Frank interrupted glancing at Kalvin behind him who shook his head no, quickly adding, "but you first"

"Thank you." She stated simply "If I knew a word that expressed it more I would use it. Um, grateful, indebted anything. Thank you for being there through everything, through my condition, through my mood swings, through every moment I should never have put you through. Through all my random adventures and through this, and what happened out there. Thank you, thank you for being there for me even when I wasn't there for you. Thank you for being the brother I never knew I wanted. So, just, thank you. Thank you."

"Don't mention it, sis" he said smiling, he knew through everything she was grateful, it just wasn't the time or place to say it "Now go to bed, or to him" and he kissed the top of her head like they'd grown up together and it was the most natural thing. There was an unusual bond there, something more than friendship, but not love. Some people believe friends of opposite sex cannot be just friends but Chrys and Frank could argue.

Frank walked past Kalvin, patted his shoulder, and went to bed. In his mind she never needed to say thanks, he knew it was there. He also knew that right now her life was complicated. He knew her secrets, her fears, her wishes and her deepest thought, because he was her best friends, as she is his. Maybe to others it wasn't so obvious but it was to him. She was his sister if not by blood by the very nature of brotherly love. And he was her brother, she loved him with every inch of her heart that was saved for the brother she always knew she needed.

Soon after they all found sleep, and sleep brought them all relief but from very different tribulations. But, for Chrys sleep for the last few years had been terrifying. She hated to close her eyes to the darkness, for everyday she feared letting her eyes fall forever to the darkness. That night, however, was distinctive and peaceful; she didn't fight sleep but gently let its hand cradle her.

That night she dreamt of the waterfall. The gleaming waters, the reflection of the moon light on the broken glass surface of the waters. She dreamt of her hand sliding across the waters. Each drip plunging deep in, sliding her troubles off along with them. Cleansing her of the mess within. Cleaning her of the sins of her parents, the sins of her body. Stripping her of the evil within her. Ending the feuding, the war that had ever waged inside her body.

They woke the next morning to a scratching sound at the door. Their door was woven of grasses and flexible stalks, so there was slits that were big enough to see through. Chrys woke up, as her and the girls' room was closest to the door. She walked to the door and peered out the slats to see a baby monkey screaming and scratching at the door. She wasn't exactly sure what to do so she ran to get Kalvin and Frank, but the monkey's screams woke them up already. Fearing it was Chrys they were running out when Chrys met them.

"A monkey! There's a baby monkey outside our door and I couldn't see the mom! What do we do?" She said running back and sticking her head out the window, they covered them with shirts they tied up. Curtains were yet to be made.

"Oh, I found the mom, something got her, and she's dead." Chrys said sadly, "Well, we can't let it die, bring it in"

"Bring it in?! Are you crazy?" Frank asked, "Haven't you ever heard of animals killing people?"

"Not baby ones whose mothers are killed and will starve without us. Plus it will know where food is, and ours isn't going to last forever and we've still got a good month, month and a half before we're supposed to be back, I don't even know."

"Fine," Frank said reaching out side and scooping the baby up when it wasn't looking. It screamed and squirmed for a minutes until Chrys wrapped it in a blanket and held it close to her.

"Aww" Marianne cooed when she saw it, "What's its name?"

"I don't know, it doesn't have one. I don't even know if it's a boy or girl" Chrys said "I'll check....it's a girl

"Aw she's so cute, and her face is all rosy colored." Marybeth said

"That's it, we'll call her Rosey!" Marianne told her
"Does she need to drink like milk or something?" Marianne asked which made Chrys remember the waterfall

"I don't know but, I found a spot where we can keep things cool. It's like what they did in the Boxcar Kids. We put the stuff behind a waterfall, come look!"

Leaving the monkey shut up in the house the group makes their way down to the waterfall. Chrys stops them where the bridge is. She shows them the cave behind the waterfall and sends the girls for the perishables. Once they return she tries to step on the first ladder step, nearly breaking it. It was the first ladder she made and the material was weak from the sun drying the mud to fast, and not getting a good stick with it.

"Marianne you try it and we'll toss you the food." she said and Marianne stepped on and slowly made her way over. They tossed her meat and dairy.

****

It was early morning Chrys and Kalvin had snuck out. They went to find more animals, larger ones to ride on. Maybe some more to help them in some way, they didn't really know.

They walked for a few hours before coming across an area of cleared land; they crouched down behind a large rock, for shade and safety. It wasn't long before the heard a loud half-roaring type noise. Kalvin peered over the rock running was an odd animal; he couldn't exactly see what it was form where they were.

It grew close and Chrys peered over, it was obvious then that it was an injured horse. Chrys stepped out and the horse ran back a few yards. It was young but its back leg. Something had attacked it. Chrys just sat down she held her hand out to Kalvin to 'say stay where you are'. She waited for the horses' curiosity to get the best of it. Eventually it came over and sniffed her head. At this point Kalvin had moved around the back of the horse. When it stopped to sniff Chrys, again he jumped it. He grabbed its main and threw himself on its back. It freaked out and flailed around nearly knocking

46

Chrys in the head. She ran and stood on the top of the rock they had hidden behind. After a few minutes of flailing and bucking, it finally gave up. Kalvin was strong and it was injured.

He rode it over to Chrys and she rubbed its nose, and eventually slid on its back with Kalvin.

"Are you sure it can hold both of us?" she whispered

"Um, yea" Kalvin said, not really sure

"Okay." Chrys said wrapping her arms around his waist.

They rode further for a while and eventually came upon more woods and the weird yowling they had heard a couple nights back. The horse froze and Kalvin slipped off. He walked very lightly over into a bush where subsequently he found a bird-like animal. Carefully he grabbed it and shoved it in his sack, which Marianne had made for hauling fruits. Motioning to Chrys to come get it carefully she rode the horse over and grabbed the bird-sack. Kalvin made his way into the bush further; he came upon a wounded wolf thing. It growled and snarled at him but he made his way behind it. It was young and small and had a pretty badly torn up back. *It defiantly lost a fight*, Kalvin thought. As he quietly made his way around the injured beast, he contemplated a plan to grab the thing, when out of nowhere Chrys, the horse and the bird bag rode in. she galloped and trampled back and forth. While at the same time, Kalvin grabbed vines and wrapped them around the flailing beast. Haling him onto the horses back Chrys rode off in front of him, showing off her formal riding lessons.

"Hey, bet you can't ride like this" she teased riding around him.

"Yea, yea let's see you wrangle a wild horse" he told her playfully chasing the horse.

"Oh, you had it easy, its hurt!" she teased as she commanded the stallion to sprint faster.

They made their way back to the hut to find Marianne making breakfast.

"Where did you too go?" Frank asked raising a teasing eye.

"Look outside" Chrys taunted, with an air of mystery.

Frank and the twins made their way over to the window and outside the saw a bag, a tied up injured wolf and an injured horse.

"Great, you go out to get animals and you come back with the worst thing in whole jungle. I mean we're stranded on an island and that's the best you can do?" Marybeth scoffed and Chrys just ignored her.

"We're gonna need somewhere to put the wolf, and horse." Chrys said, as she climbed back down and got the bird bag, "and windows to keep the monkey and bird in"

"I swear we fell into a movie cause this couldn't get any weirder, maybe someone out there is just watching us and making a novel out of our lives." Marybeth said

Glancing at Marybeth, Chrys, Kalvin and Frank went to work building. They cleared out and area around the bottom of the tree, in a big circle. They built a type of fencing, keeping the animals in and out. It went up a good 4 feet in fencing the the rest of the way, another 3 feet in a mesh of vines and stalks. They then set to work building walls around the back of the base of the tree trunk. They built walls, and knowing that it was safe now to work into the night they did. Eventually the whole thing was finished by the break of dawn. As Chrys put the finishing touches on the doors and feeding troughs, she wove the animals were lead in the horse first. They set it in is stall and Chrys go to work bandaging up its leg, so it could walk without any problems. Then they carried the growling wolf in. Unsure of the nature of the beast Chrys worked carefully wrapping its back and leg with bandages. Eventually she let the great creatures legs go. She sat with it a while, trying to calm it down and let it know it could trust her. Then when she felt like the animal was tranquil, she slowly undid its mouth harnesses. She walked out quietly, making sure not to scare him. She had named him Trek, because she felt like he had gone through a lot and trek means to go long distances. The horse was beautiful, strong, and proud she felt like it needed a name that went with the wind. Something that showed its nature to run with the wind and chase the birds. So she named it Zephyr, which is a soft, gentle breeze. Climbing back up to the hut, she noticed Marianne and Marybeth had made shutters out of woven board fastened to the side of the hut. She climbed in and immediately she was bombarded with questions after politely answering all of them she learned they had named the bird Pookie II, after the bird they had at home. She had Frank and Kal make stalls and such for the bird and monkey and put them down there too. She then made her way to the bedroom, exhausted she fell into a deep sleep. Out in the other room Kalvin just sat. Frank went to see the animals and so did the twins, but Kalvin just sat. For some odd reason he couldn't put his finger on he felt suddenly depressed and alone. He knew he wasn't alone Chrys was there but he just kept thinking she's gonna leave me all alone, I'll be all alone. He stared at the makeshift door of the girls' room. He wandered over to the door almost without realizing it. Leaning his head on the door, he felt the change, he felt something go away, to go back to before. He knew he couldn't go back to that, to the feeling he got when he first fell in love. He couldn't call it love that was dangerous. It made her death terrifying. He wasn't one to be scared, he'd done and seen so much he shouldn't get scared but he was he was petrified. He slowly opened the door and sat by her on the floor. He could remember the last time he had the same feeling as if it was yesterday. Her chemo stopped working and she got worse and worse. He remembered her looking at him through tired eyes. Just staring as she slowly slipped away. He remembered the cold of her hand as she stroked his face. As she slowly slipped away he remembered dying inside, just losing everything he had. So he sobbed. He sobbed then and he wanted to now. He wasn't sure why this time, she was alive he could see it. He just touched her, ran his hand along her face. Slowly she turned over to face him. She smiled and with tired eyes, reached up to him. She scotched over and patted the bed.

"Chrys," he said sitting next to her "are you getting sick again?"

She sighed knowing inside the answer wasn't good. And it wasn't certain either. He wrapped his arms around her waist as they sat propped against the wall. She turned under his arms and laid her head on his chest, holding his shirt tight in her hands.

"I don't know Kal. I'm getting that feeling again." She whispered

His heart sank and he squeezed her tighter, kissed her head and prayed it wasn't true.

"Life never works out does it?" he whispered not for her to hear but just a confirmation in his mind.

"Yes, it does," she told him "you only see the bad but I can see the good. I see that my cancer and your mistakes are a good thing."

"How could they possibly be good?" he asked pulling the blanket over her

"If I hadn't had cancer I wouldn't have gone to bail my cousin out that day and if you hadn't done what you did you never would've run into me. Do you see? Life is a tricky thing, that's what I've learned from all of this. It gives you the bad to produce the good. God doesn't just throw bad things at people, he has a reason for everything. He knows what's going to happen in the end, but we can always change it, we can always make a different decision and it may or may not work out, but that's the most wonderful part. I made the decision that my family didn't need any more heartache so I went to get my cousin. God knows I should've let him stay in there to teach him a lesson but I think he learned one anyway. Seeing you scared him more than jail could've. So don't you see it all worked out in the end. It brought us here and I thank God everyday for that. Now, don't make that face. This island is a miracle in disguise. Without it, I think nothing between us would've ever changed. Kalvin, can't- won't you- see? So if I get sick again something good will come of it, I promise."

"But, Chrys, I-I can't lose you."

"I'll never leave, not really. Even if I can't stay on this earth I'll always be with you, just know so long as you are alive I'll be watching. See Kalvin the thing is-"

"I love you." Kalvin blurted

"I-I" Chrys stammered

"It's true I do." Kalvin said

"Well then Kalvin what I was going to say makes even more sense. Love is a funny thing; it strikes in the weirdest ways. You may not see it coming, you may not want to but it comes, trust me. It tells that even with everything going on in your life, everything that you did or should have good things are still coming. You're still worthy. That somebody will always be on your side, and will always care about you. Someone is going to believe in you and it may be naive but I believe in fairy tales. They might not be straight out of the book but it's still a fairy tale. And all fairy tales have happy endings."

"Not everybody deserves a princess though."

"No, and not every princess wants a prince charming either."

****

"Come on, it's about time we have some fun around this place!" Kalvin shouted jumping off of the waterfall.

"Woohoo!" Frank hollered following

"Not happening" Marianne warned Marybeth

"Oh, yes it is" she said pulling Marianne off with her

Chrys unsure if she had the strength to do that and not wanting to alarm her friends or ruin the fun jumped. Screaming the whole way down. Plunging deep below the water, the cool water let way to relief of her pain. So she stayed under for a while. She knew she alarmed Kalvin when she saw him dive under. She waved and he laughed. She came up and swam over to them. She floated on her back for a while, listened to Marianne and Marybeth splash around, and play for a bit. Kalvin swam under her grabbed her waist and pulled her under. She freaked out a bit before she realized it was him. He let her go and she swam back up. That's when he saw the bruises on her back. His face just turned white.

"What's wrong?" she asked

"Your back, the bruises."

"Don't worry it's probably just from jumping" she said passing it off and to him it made sense or he wanted it to. It had to, that had to be it. He just nodded and she knew she was lying and he knew she was lying. But there could be no other explanation. They had to believe that she was healed.

"Quit worrying and let's have some fun!" she said quickly changing the subject.

****

It wasn't true though, she wasn't healed and there's doubt she ever had been. In her mind, it was one big glaring lie, one huge lie to shut her up. Probably orchestrated to ease her feelings because the end would come fast. *Well,* she thought, *news flash docs I've never done anything by the book with this.* She had no proof of this but when she thought back on a miracle healing it just isn't true, it just doesn't happen. She felt silly even thinking it could. It was just too hard for anyone to accept the truth. The truth hurts people and no one wants to die knowing they caused so much pain. She'd said this a lot, she'd helped with other kids a lot. She gave them hope and comfort in their last days and now they turned the tables. But, no way is she giving up that easily. *I'm a fighter and that's exactly what I'll die doing. I'm tired of hurting, I'm tired of hurting people and I'm damn tired of this disease!*

She looked around and she was suddenly so aware of how alone she was. There was just them on this island. *I'm gonna die here and no one will ever know. No, shut up Chrys! The only thing I have to fear is fear itself.* She wasn't exactly sure who said that but she knew it was painted on her bedroom wall at home. She also knew that the hospital wall said, "You're never truly alone until you abandon yourself." Until then she never really understood what it meant. She didn't get that it meant the only way people will give up on you recovering is if you give up yourself to the disease. It was a revelation in her mind she realized although science plays a huge part in her healing her own state of mind ultimately decides what happens. If she gives up then hallelujah for the disease but if, she doesn't then on with the fight. She imagined little soldiers walking into the night to fight for her. She just smiled and thought *my soldiers never lose*.

****

Chrys thought it funny now that for so long in her life she fought herself to feel pretty. Pretty doesn't matter in the end. All the trivial things she'd worried about mean nothing. Most people can't see that until the very end of their lives when their little old people but she gets a sneak peak. She'll know how much every day means to her. She'll know how much her family and friends mean to her. Frivolous are the woes of a young girl's existence. Disease brings end to all frivolous simplicity nevertheless emits wisdom and an absolute comprehension of humanity. Innocence however is continuously seized too soon.

****

"Is, that a...boat?" Chrys asked Kalvin as they stood at the top of the waterfall one day.

"Holy...shit! A boat!" they began running gathering their friends as they went.

They ended up at the beach, where they soon realized the boat was a lot closer than they thought, and a lot smaller. It wasn't for them, they hadn't been gone long enough. Well, they weren't exactly sure how long it had been but they thought it wasn't long enough. They stood waving but no one answered them. When the boat approached land, they realized that something was very wrong. It wasn't slowing down and they couldn't see anyone on it. Running back, they watched as it crashed to land.

"No!" Marybeth yelled "That was supposed to take us home!"

Chrys ran towards it Kalvin and Frank in tow. Climbing the side ladder and hopping below they searched for people only to find no one. They double, triple checked, and no one was there.

"This is a problem, there could be people out in the ocean." She told them, "We need to swim out a little and check."

"No way! You are staying on dry land!" Kalvin told her "I'll go out."

"You're not going alone. Frank, will you *please* go with him?" she asked sticking her bottom lip out playfully

"Yes" he said playfully pushing her shoulder. Not wanting to waste time, they decided not to go back for bathing suits. Swimming out to see if there were people sounded easier than it was. The waves were towering and violent that day. They pounded and beat them until they didn't think they could go any further, but hearing the cries kept them going. About 4 yards out, they heard what sounded like a small child crying about 3 yards ahead. Pausing momentarily to catch their breath, they decided they had to keep going. In total, it took them about 20 minutes to make it out to the stranded group. Once out there they gathered three young girls. Kalvin put the oldest and the youngest girl on his back, Frank taking the middle child. They swam back and collapsed on the beach. Chrys and the twins rushed over.

"Are you okay?" Chrys asked Kalvin and he nodded, she was worried about him putting too much effort forward, doing more than his body could handle. He was powerfully built but still he couldn't do everything.

She half crawled half walked over to where they dropped the girls.

"Are you okay?" she asked the middle child, who they had let go first.

She nodded and asked, "Who are you?" in a raspy voice.

"My name is Chrys, now don't talk too much" she told the young girl moving onto the oldest sister

"Are you okay? Did you swallow a lot of water?" she asked kindly

"No, I'm fine!" the girl snapped sitting up "Where is my boat? And who are you?!"

"I'm Chrys and your boat is over there, but it's not gonna get you far there's a giant hole in it!" Chrys shouted to her as the girl ran over to the boat. It seemed odd that the boat was more important than the little girls were.

"Hi sweetie," Chrys said picking up the littlest girl "Are you okay?"

The little girl was crying and shaking.

"It's okay sweetie, shh, it's okay" Chrys comforted her as the other little girl crawled over to her.

"Hon, can you tell me what happened. Who you are? Anything?" Chrys asked as the middle girl scooted closer to Chrys.

"I'm Sammy and this is my little sister Jennie. I'm eight and she's three" the little girl explained "That is our big sister, Lela, from the big sister progwam. Please don't make us go back with her."

"Aww, sweetie it'll be okay, I promise." She said as the young girls huddled in her lap.

"We've got no mommy or daddy" Sammy told her as Chrys stroked her hair. "They call us orpans"

"Orphans?" she asked and they young girl nodded.

"She's rich, rich peoples are meanies!" Sammy said as Chrys walked with her hand-in-hand.

"Not all rich people are mean. I'm a rich person and I'm not mean, right?" Chrys asked and the small girl pulled away, tears forming in her eyes.

"Are you gonna hit me, now?" she asked Chrys.

"Hit you? No, of course not sweetheart. Does someone hit you?" Chrys asked bending down on her knees, the half-sleeping toddler on her hip.

"I'm not apposed to tell you." Sammy said looking back at Lela

"Don't worry I won't tell on you, I promise." Chrys said pinky promising the scared little girl.

"Mrs. Stacey does and she says it okay if Lela does, too. But I never apposed to tell." Sammy said holding tight to Chrys's hip.

"It's okay Sammy, sweetie, we won't hurt you, I promise. You trust me right?" Chrys asked and she nodded yes.

"Come on honey, let's get you cleaned up okay?" and they walked back over to the group.

"This is Sammy, she's eight and this is her sister Jennie-"Chrys stated

"She's three!" Sammy interrupted

"Yes, she is!" Chrys laughed whispering "they're orphans" aside to Frank and Kalvin she added "abused orphans."

"They want to stay with us. So be nice." She told poking Maryanne and Marybeth's shoulders.

"We will." They said together, going around they introduced themselves. When Kalvins turn came he tried to be extra nice, because he came across so scary to people. A brawny, tattoo covered former gang-member would scare a lot of people. But Sammy just saw the guy that saved her. She went right over and wrapped her arms as far around his waist as they could go.

Kalvin looked up at Chrys and she just smiled at him.

"Hey! What are you two doing?" Lela yelled running over and grabbing Sammy by the arm yanking her away from Kalvin.

"Let me go!" Sammy screamed

"I'm sorry; my sisters are a little crazy sometimes. Sam stop!" she said yanking at the girls arm. Chrys couldn't help but think, *damn your good...but not good enough*.

"I don't think you're going anywhere with her!" Chrys said yanking her hand off of Sammy's arm and she ran behind her.

"Excuse me but that's my little sister!" Lela said shocked.

"Kal, Frank please remove her!" Chrys said and Kalvin stepped up

Frank was mesmerized, Lela was beautiful. Long dark hair, tanned skin perfect hourglass shape.

"Frank!" Chrys yelled, he looked at her.

"Chrys she says there her sisters let her have them!"

"I believe Sammy and you should believe me!" she said her voice rising, all this yelling caused both girls to cry.

"Okay, stop!" Kalvin shouted "All of you! Until we can figure out what is going on they are staying with us in the hut and she is staying on the boat now Chrys take them and get their stuff off the boat and we're leaving, that is final!"

"A guy who can put his foot down is kinda hot..." the girl said trying to flirt her way into getting what she wanted.

"Back off!" Chrys told her simultaneously with Kalvin, as she passed by them.

****

Later that night Chrys sat up in the living room with Kalvin and his tomahawk thing Frank made waiting for Lela to come and try to take them or sabotage them in some way.

"I'm worried, we don't have enough food for them to stay forever and the little one has two pairs of clothes and a binky. And Marybeth already hates me enough as it is..."

"I don't hate you, sissy." Marybeth said walking out and sitting between Chrys's legs with her back to Chrys. Chrys wrapped her arms around her sister's waist. "I'm sorry I'm such a brat sometimes. I know you love me."

"Do you?" Chrys asked

"Yes, we both do especially Marianne, probably because when we were little and she was so sick they thought she wouldn't walk or talk but you knew she would. That's why she never gets mad at you because she's knows you love her and believe in her always, even when bad things happen. I can't always remember that." Marybeth told her, turning sideways looking up at her big sister. Chrys kissed her forehead.

"I love you, Bethy" she said and Marybeth nodded tears rolling down her cheeks.

"I'm sorry if I made you cry" Beth said.

"Don't worry the past is gone, just know I'll love you always." Chrys told her and Marybeth turned to Kalvin who immediately turned away.

"Kalvin, I'm sorry that I'm bad sometimes and I yell and...yeah" she said and he smiled and said

"Me too, kid, me too." And she hugged his neck.

"Go to bed." Chrys told her.

"Can I sleep out here?" she asked.

"Yea" Chrys told her as she ran to get her blanket and pillow.

****

"Chrys?" Marianne hollered running out sometime later.

"Anne, what's wrong?" Chrys said sitting up from where she was lying, Marybeth on one side Kalvin on the other.

"I had a dream that, that lady came and I woke up and you were dead." She said sobbing and falling into her arms.

"Marianne, it was just a dream, kid it's okay." Kalvin said running his hand down her hair trying to be kinder in his words.

"You won't let I happen right?" she asked him.

"No, kid everybody will be okay, promise." He told her and she nodded. She scooted over near Kalvin holding onto his arm while Chrys got her blanket. That night they slept, except for Kalvin. Kalvin on the outside, then Marianne, Chrys and finally Marybeth, the twins sharing Chrys's arms and chest.

****

The next morning they all woke, up and took to their respective chores. The twins went out to get the food, Kalvin took to the animals and Chrys washed their clothes.

But, Chrys knew trouble was brewing in more way than one. Large dark storm clouds rolled in from the ocean. They ran back to the hut shoving sand up as far as they could in front of the makeshift barn. When they got sand, a good ways up the sides they ran up the ladder, buckling down the hatch. Closing doors, putting up half made shutters. Anything to keep the water out and the hut together. Over the past few days, Frank and Kalvin had been working on a storm cover for the hut and barn. They put the finished one over the hut and the half finished over the barn. The storm cover was made out of the strongest branches or trees woven together with straw and stalks plastered with mud-glue. They made it as domed as they could. Chrys and Kalvin fastened it down with mud and rock covered with mud-glue. It turns out the half-finished one fit perfectly covering just the barn leaving the "pasture" uncovered. After taking care of everything they could they hauled food and wood up. Gathering in the living room with blankets and pillows and a warm fire Chrys tried to ease their fears with stories and pretending it was camping. Although she pretended, it was just a thunderstorm she was scared of what it could really be. Hurricane, tsunami, their hut couldn't with stand them. And Frank, where was Frank? He wasn't there when she woke up, she figured he woke up early and got started working again, but he wasn't back yet. As the four girls sat and ate their lunch. Kalvin sat with his girl.

"Where's Frank?" they asked at the same time

Chrys looked out the hatch in the storm cover for him and shook her head no. She tried to hide how scared she really was but Kalvin could tell and he just held her in his arms as they sat there.

He kissed her head as the thunder started and the baby cried. Crawling to Chrys Jennie held her arms out and crying said

"Up-y"

Holding the scared little girl in her arms, they all huddled in the corner. Kalvin with his arm around Chrys and Marianne curled up on his other side. Chrys with Jennie in her lap, Sammy in between her and Marybeth who was on the other side. The hut shook and they could hear the animals growling and whinnying below them. Knowing they were a lightning strikes best friend Chrys had covered the storm covers with as much mud-plaster as she could. Lightening light up the sky through the cracks in the shutters, on the windows, in the storm cover they could see it. Rain poured down and once Chrys was sure it was just a really bad thunderstorm they watched from a safe distance through the cracks.

"This is so cool!" Marybeth said and Chrys laughed. A loud, deep scream echoed through their walls then.

Chrys immediately looking at Kalvin, who shook his head, ran out under the storm cover to crack the door a bit. She screamed when she saw Frank on the ground his leg underneath a tree branch. Kalvin, hearing her scream, ran out to see what was wrong.

"Chrys, Chrys are you okay?" he asked as she buried her head in his chest and pointed behind her.

"God, damn him! Stay here I'll go get him." He said climbing down the ladder. The storm cover had a door and two windows where the windows in the hut were.

Chrys ran back in and collapsed onto the floor.

"Chrys!" Marianne exclaimed.

"Annie, I'm fine, really. It's okay." Chrys said laying her head on the girls' shoulder, tears sneaking from her eyes.

****

"Ah! Damn it, Frank!" Kalvin said trying to lift the log off of his leg "What did you do?"

"I didn't do anything! Ahh! Damn!" he said as Kalvin slid the log along his leg.

"Sorry" Kalvin said trying to lift it, "I can't lift it!"

"But dude-" Frank said moaning in pain.

"I know, but it's a tree!" Kalvin argues as he slid it off of Frank's leg.

"Ah! Is it bad?" Frank asked

"Nah, it doesn't look broken or anything." Kalvin said helping him to his feet.

"Ahh!!" Frank grunted as he tried to put weight on his leg "God damn it!"

"Next time don't be so damn stupid." Kalvin said under his breath

After what seemed like eternity, Chrys heard them slip under the storm cover as the thunder rumbled above. She stood and waited as they came inside and Frank sat by the door.

"*Ohmigod*! Are you okay?" Chrys asked sitting next to him, taking his hand.

"Yea I'm fine, really." He said as she pulled his pant leg up.

"Holy-"she started to say as the baby crawled over "moly"

"Ah! That bad?" he asked squeezing her hand

"Yes, that bad, what were you doing?" she asked rummaging around for the first aid kit.

"Ouch da-rn it" he said trying to be careful not to use foul language as the baby was there.

"I'm sorry" Chrys said patching up his leg the best she knew how. Holding her arm to numb the pain, Frank left finger marks.

"Sorry, it hurts" he said petting her arm over the marks.

"No, it's okay" she told him scooting up closer and throwing her arms around his shoulders. He laid his head on her shoulder and she stroked his head. They stayed like that for a while until she needed to make dinner. At some point, it dawned on her that Kalvin wasn't out there anymore.

"Kal? Kalvin! Kalvin!?" she called out the window.

****

"Oh hell no! She is gonna kill him." Kalvin said walking the path he assumed Frank walked earlier. The thunder roaring above him he knew he didn't have much time. The footprints, what were left of them anyway, lead towards the shore. Towards Lela. He couldn't help but think of how Frank warned him never to hurt her and now he was. As quietly as he could he snuck up on the boat where Lela was holed up.

"Shit!" Kalvin said as lightening struck a tree not far from him, instantly setting it in flames. As fast as he possibly could he sprinted back to the hut. Entering the storm cover, he found Chrys tending to Frank but peering out to look for him at the same time.

"Kal!" she said throwing her arms around his shoulders, he looked at Frank intensely as he hugged her.

Damn, was all Frank could think, he hoped and prayed he hadn't gone out there to look for where he had been. Chrys was right in her feeling beforehand something was afoot. Something bad and it was gonna blow and blow hard.

The storm carried on through the night shaking the house and keeping them all in the living room until the kids fell asleep and so did Chrys.

"Frank, what the hell were you doing out there?" Kalvin whispered to him. Chrys fell asleep with the baby behind her and spooning with Marianne. Sammy came after that followed by Marybeth who was practically chocking the little girl the way she was holding her. Kalvin reached over and removed her arms from the poor little thing. He then moved the baby onto a stack of blankets and covered her, moving her by Marybeth, then moved behind Chrys in her spot. Frank stayed by the door.

"Where were you?" Kalvin whispered from where he was sitting.

"What?" Frank asked, not really sure of what to think.

"*Where were you?*" repeated Kalvin.

"When?" Frank asked, stalling.

"*Damn, Frank tell m*e. I'm not stupid and neither is she. If I can figure it out so will she." Kalvin demanded.

"Just out seeing the damage." He lied.

"During the storm?" Kalvin asked.

"Damn, Kal back off, okay? Just back off."

"Or *what?*" Kalvin demanded knowing that if Frank were to use violence or brute strength he wouldn't get too far or off the hook.

"I'll tell" Frank warned hoping that would be the end of it but knowing better than that

"Tell what?" Kal challenged.

"*The Secret.*" Frank said softly. Praying Kalvin wouldn't call his bluff. Partly he knew he would and partly he knew he wouldn't. His nature is to confront and fight, never give up until you win or you're dead is his motive. But, he had a lot to lose and he would if anyone ever knew.

Kalvin hesitated for a second, in situations like this the quote-un-quote old Kalvin would've just decked him and been done with it. He couldn't though, he couldn't take that chance.

"I...I won't tell her but you have to or I'll tell her *The Secret* myself."

Frank in some way got what he wanted and what he feared most. Kalvin both called his bluff and gave in. The prospect of having her know either where he was *or The Secret* now rested with him. And Kalvin had a lot more to lose from it. Frank couldn't help but wonder if it was a bluff or if he would really give everything up to keep his secret.

Inside Kalvin was in a panic but outside he remained calm. He knew, *knew* that Frank would never let him do that. *Right?* But, wherever he was and whatever he was actually doing had to be pretty bad to blow *The Secret* on it. Either way they all lost. Neither thing should exist, Franks secret or *The Secret.* Kal should've known though, that it was too good to be true. Someone like him couldn't get something that perfect. Fate, and whatever else was out there, conspired against him the second he pulled that trigger, the second they all did.

****

Eventually the storm wound down and they needed to survey the damage. They went out, patched up the holes in the storm cover, and fixed the fence down around the animal pasture. Chrys could sense that something was wrong. She could just feel it. It was as if the air whispered it in her ear. The birds in the trees called it down to her. And the animals scurrying around warned her of the problem.

"I... think we should go check on the girl." Chrys said breaking the ominous silence

Frank's face went from his normal color to red to white within seconds. And the sudden change didn't escape Chrys's silent eye.

They followed her there in silence, it was a bad situation and she didn't know it. To break the silence Chrys decided they should play a game.

"Confession?" she asked.

"Okay" Kal said softly.

"My full name is Chrystal" Chrys said, "I haven't used it since like 2nd grade."

"Your turn" Chrys said.

"Uh, I lied, I wasn't 15 when I joined the gang I was 12." Kal said "15 seems better, out of the worse."

"Frank..." Kal said as they approached the boat.

****

"Sammy, we have a lot of work to do. Chrys and Kalvin are like in love or something so I figured we'd crown them king and queen of this island." Marybeth said in a childlike way.

"But, to be king and queen they have to be married" Marianne told her "So we have to do that first"

"What's the islands name?" Sammy asked.

"Um, Robinson Island" Marianne said.

"Perfet let's go" Sammy said smiling.

****

"What do you want?!" the girl screamed coming out of the wreckage of her boat.

"We came to see if you were ok" Chrys said as they girl kept glancing back and forth between her and Frank. At this point, he was staring at the ground, his hands sweating profusely.

"I'm fine now go away or give me the kids back so I can leave." She said shoving her back, causing her to lose her balance. Not wanting to cause a fight Chrys decided it was time to leave. They walked in silence for a bit before Chrys took up the cause again. She hated awkward silences.

"Frank confession" she demanded as they walked away.

"I don't know." He lied

"There has to be something you want to confess you're not perfect. You have to have some secret; I mean really, who doesn't have at least one secret. I have secrets. How don't you?"

"Okay, you know you're so hell bent on the truth I'll tell you!" Frank blurted harshly getting shocked and warning looks. But he didn't stop.

"The truth is I didn't go out for any of the reason you think I did! I went out-," Frank was yelling

"Stop!" Kalvin said pushing him backward away from Chrys "Shut up!"

"No let go of me!" Frank yelled

"Frank you don't know what you're doing." He hissed below his breath

"Yes, I do." Frank told him pushing back

"You'll blow everything!" Kalvin said his heart racing "I can't protect you."

"I don't need protecting, *you do*! I won't protect you anymore." Frank whispered.

"Frank don't!" Kal said his breathing picking up "Please."

Frank just shook his head and pushed past him. Kal just let him go, in the face of losing everything he let him go. It almost stopped Frank too; it almost made him turn around. But he didn't and Kal just stood there shocked. He turned around and ran over to Chrys all he did was shake his head and whisper

"I always loved you."

"What?" she said, everything was spinning. For one second Frank almost thought it best to stop. He almost thought, how could I do this to her, she loves him. He loves her. Secrets are secrets for a reason. But he didn't he just stood and waited for the question.

"What's going on?" Chrys asked.

****

Kalvin walked away slowly at first then faster and by the time, he was out of sight he was running. His heart was pounding out of his chest and he could barely breathe. He stopped above the waterfall and simply looked over. For the first time, in what seemed like forever but truly wasn't, he let the tears slip from his eyes. His only thoughts were *Please don't let her hate me...I love her.* I love her, he had to say it aloud to realize the weight of it. His tears slipped into the water as he whispered "I love you Chrystal...I always will." He knew she would hate him, he could feel it. He knew he deserved it too, but she didn't. She took a chance on a lost cause and lost. The tears got heavier, and he began to shake as he fell to his knees. He prayed, like he never prayed before. But he didn't pray for her forgiveness or for Frank to stop, he prayed she would know how much he loved her and that her hurt wouldn't last long. He prayed that for every minute of her hurt he got a year of his own hurt.

****

She felt like dying, every word that slipped from Frank's mouth stung her. It felt as if a violent wind of betrayal cut her down with every brutal slap. Her hands began to shake her mind spinning. *Why is he doing this to me?! It's not fair; he couldn't just let me go happily.*

"Frank stop talking, just stop." Chrys said softly, but he couldn't hear her he was just yelling. Spewing the truth. "Frank, it's back, the disease. Frank I'm dying"

He just wouldn't listen to her; he kept going and going and going. Finally, she knew there was only one way to prove it. She lifted her shirt up over her head and he continued to talk until she turned around. He stopped in the middle of his sentence and just stared. The bruises, he knew what the bruises meant. The bruises meant that the tumors were growing again. They started in her spine and then moved to her lungs, followed by her heart then her brain.

"Chrys," he said, "Chrys, please tell me that- no. No, no no!"

At this point, she was crying. She slipped her shirt back on as he wrapped her in his arms.

"What did I do?" he whispered to himself, "I'm sorry. I'm so sorry. Go find him."

She looked up at her big brother and he smiled. It couldn't get any worse. He just ruined the rest of her life. If they weren't found, she would die there and he just ruined everything. She left then, she ran as fast as she could. Frank just sat there trying to understand why he did that to her. He couldn't remember then what would ever possess him to hurt her. He loved her, she was his sister.

"Kal! Kalvin! Kal, where are you?" he heard her coming and wanted to hide but he couldn't move. He just stayed where he was on his knees.

"Kal" she said softly "What are you doing?"

He just sat there, she could see him breathing. He seemed so different, so small. She couldn't wrap her head around the idea that he was the same guy she just heard about. But, then again, he wasn't. He had changed a lot and she knew it. She watched him change she changed with him.

"I told you once that no matter what you had done it didn't matter to me. You've changed your life. Kal, I love you no matter what. It hasn't changed and it won't." she whispered laying her hand on his shoulder.

He stood up taking her hand. He stared deep into her eyes and for the first time he realized how much this tiny sick little girl really meant to him. But, he couldn't take it back it was done and there was nothing he could do to make it better.

"Kal, you need to come back with me, please. I can't go out like this. I need you to love me." She pleaded.

"I would never stop." He said softly

"Please, just move on it's okay. The past is the past for a reason. It's not to be dwelled on. What we have here and now is what's important. We have love and I'm not leaving until I know that it will be the same as it was that night you first told me."

"It won't- it can't be." he told her "But, different isn't always bad." He didn't know if he could ever be okay with hurting her but he loved her and he couldn't lose her. If this was how he got to keep her, he had to take it, even if everything in his being told him to leave her alone- he couldn't. Kal hugged her as close to himself as he could. Telling himself it would all work out and trying to pretend he believed it, too.

"I'm sorry" he told her " I know you don't wanna hear it but I need to tell you what happened that night. It's important to me. No more secrets, okay? I won't lie to you again. I swear. You mean too much." He paused here then added "I love you so much."

"I know you do," she whispered kissing his cheek "so tell me if you need to."

****

"Are we done?" Marianne asked

"Yepp that's everythin." Marybeth said

"We need to get dressed up!" Marianne said suddenly "and fast. I've got Sammy."

"Okay, go." They said taking them and trying to get them to look as fancy as possible. They brushed their hair and tried to put it up as best they could.

****

Frank decided he'd caused enough damage for the day so he headed back to the hut. He never guessed they would be on their way back too, not yet. He hoped he would

67

avoid them, at least for a while. Until Kal calmed down, because he couldn't be happy. But they were there and Kal didn't look happy to see him.

Chrys's heart was pounding when she saw Frank coming. She held Kal's hand tighter and tired to keep him from doing anything. But he broke away and headed straight toward Frank. Chrys tired to call to him but nothing came out. Frank smiled at her and she mouthed 'I'm sorry for whatever happens' and he nodded. Kal stood directly in front of him neither of them said anything for a while. Frank eventually said

"If your gonna take your shot do it"

Kal just shook his head and held out his hand. Frank stood confused for a second, he thought if nothing else he would take at least one shot, but nothing. Nothing. He just stood there and held his hand out. Even Chrys was confused she stared at them but she smiled and thought *I knew it. I knew he changed.* So Frank took his hand and shook it. He didn't understand how they didn't hate him. In fact, neither boy understood it. But, it just made everything peaceful.

Every anger or secret they had just seemed to disappear. They just walked back in silence but it was awkward or angry silence. Just silence. Before they got to the hut, Chrys stopped in front of them.

"I have something to say." She announced "I'm gonna tell them soon. Maybe not today but soon. They'll figure it out eventually. Promise me something though; if I die here you won't leave me when they find you."

Kal looked down then, it was hard for him to understand life without his angel. She saved his life and now he has to watch her lose hers. It doesn't seem right, but he knows he can't do anything about it. He couldn't help it, he knew he should be strong but he just didn't feel strong. He felt very small and powerless. He nodded even though.

"Okay, let's go." She said climbing up.

Frank just whispered to Kal "I'll take care of that part." At that point, there was no denying it; if they stayed much longer, she would get very sick, very fast. Kal nodded and they walked in.

"Crap" Kal said under his breath when they saw what the kids did.

"Um, uh what-what is this?" Chrys asked seeing what seemed to be a makeshift wedding ceremony.

"Your wedding" Marianne said proudly. They were dressed in the dresses Chrys made them bring just in case. Marianne pulled Chrys into the room to get her ready.

Marybeth took the boys into their room and told them to wear tuxedos. She left then, not giving them a chance to refuse. Chrys had made them all pack one dress and tux just in case they ended up doing something fancy. She never guessed it would be used for her wedding! The twins dragged the boys to their makeshift altar placing Kal in the grooms spot and Frank in the priests.

"Mary" Frank said "I'm not a priest, I can't marry them."

"Sure you can." She said "Pretend."

"Maybe- maybe you should ask them if they want to do this first." He called as she walked into Chrys's room.

"Frank, I really can't get married right now. This- this-" Kal started

"I don't know what we're supposed to do. She'll make the right decision" Frank told him as they led Chrys out of the room. They had her in the white dress she brought with a veil of flowers they wove together draped over her head. Her dress was tight on the top twisting around her until her hips where it flowed out in ripples. She wore white dresses because they make her looked darker, less pale. The flowers were many colors and landed just above her behind. Her eyes were wet behind the makeup she held a necklace in her hand. Walking up to Kal, she held out her hand. Behind her smoky eye shadow a red lipstick, she held the tears.

"We don't have to do this" she whispered as he took the necklace from her. He knew the necklace the second she held it out. He had given it to her before she almost died.

"It's up to you." He said clasping the necklace around her neck.

She looked up at him, running her hand along the necklace. It was a silver chain with a diamond encrusted C at the end. The C was intertwined with a K. She didn't know what she wanted, she knew she loved him but she also knew that this wasn't real. When they went back, if they did, it would all be fake. But, she had this sinking feeling that she might never go back and she loved him. So maybe this is her last chance. Maybe this is her blessing. Maybe God is telling her you need to do this now because I can't let them have you much longer.

"Do you want to?" she asked him.

"I don't have a ring" he whispered kissing her head.

"But, you have a necklace." She whispered taking it back off. "And I have a ring."

The ring she spoke of was the ring she got him when he graduated from school. The school he'd left many years ago and the school she tutored him through. It was silver to match her necklace with the same symbolism etched into it. He smiled and nodded handing her the ring. She didn't know he kept it with him but it never left his side.

She walked back down to the end of the aisle letting the twins go before her. Dressed in matching pale pink dresses adorned with flower halos. Followed by Sammy holding Jennie. In their makeshift dresses made from flowers and other pieces of clothing thrown together their green eyes stood out with their auburn hair. Frank who stood in the spot of the preacher smiled at Chrys as she went down the aisle, nobody was there to walk her and that's how she likes it. This is something she should do on her own. She she smiled back staring him in the eyes, his hazel eyes smiled back. He tried to brush up what was once his spiky brown hair. It was her wedding, he wanted to look nice for it. Kalvin stood there seemingly tattoo less smiling at his bride to be. Without the tattoos, she noticed how different he looked just another guy with gray eyes and black hair. But he wasn't just another guy not to her. To her he was *the guy.* The one-guy women searched for years that is perfect for them and yet hers was just handed to her. It made her wonder why but then again it didn't matter and she- for now- didn't care.

It echoed in her mind once again, *this isn't real Chrys,* but she didn't care. Little did she know that the same though flashed through Kalvin's mind and similarly he pushed it away, not aside, and not momentarily...forever.

She smiled as she took her place next to the makeshift altar. She never knew what her wedding would look like and now it couldn't be more perfect.

She stared into Kalvin's eyes there seemed to be something there she never saw before, something magical. She realized what it was and she realized she just never looked before. It was love. She wanted to reach out to him but she didn't. She felt sick. Making him do this. Marry the dead.

"You don't have to do this" she whispered, "It's not real but still..."

"No I don't have to" he told her ignoring the hurt and relief in her eyes, "But I want to. It might not be real to the US but it is to me."

He smiled and turned to Frank whispering "Go" Frank nodded glancing at Chrys who nodded. They didn't know the whole speech but it didn't matter what they had was sufficient.

"We are gathered here today to join in holy matrimony these two young people." Frank said improvising the parts, he didn't know "so, do you Kalvin Vance take you Chrystal Marks as your lawfully wedded wife to love and to hold. For better or worse. In si-" he stopped Kalvin sighed and Chrys laughed.

"In sickness and in health." She finished for him

"Til" he breathed deep "death do you part?"

"I do" his deep voice was suddenly softer and shaky. His chest heaved but his face was solid.

"You okay?" Chrys asked.

"Mhmm" he murmured.

"You sure?" she whispered and he nodded.

" Do you Chrystal Marks take you Kalvin Vance to be your lawfully wedded husband to love and to hold. In sickness and in health. Til death do you part?"

"I do" Chrys whispered then repeating it louder "I do."

"Then by the power bested in me by me I now pronounce you husband and wife. You may kiss the bride!" Frank announced throwing his hands in the air and smiling.

Kalvin took Chrys in his hands and kissed her like he'd never kissed anyone before. When he let her go, she could see the fear in his eyes but he was smiling. His breathing was still heavy. He stared at her smiling put his gaze was hard.

"Kal you okay?"

He shook his head yes but she knew he was lying. He stared at her whispering

"My angel. My precious angel." His voice shook as he reached for her running his hand along his shoulder. His hand was shaking, his eyes closed, turning his head to the side. She looked down at his hand. Then seeing the bruise she knew what was wrong.

"Kal it could- it could be-" he shook his head "It could be a fluke"

His chest was heaving so hard she thought he would explode.

"It's not." He whispered, "Check- check your ribs. It wouldn't skip a step."

She pulled the front of her dress out looking down at her ribs. She shook her head soft at first then faster.

"It's moving too fast. I should've had a few months not days. If-if I keeps up I'll be dead in two days." She closed her eyes." Kal"

"Shh" he held her close to him running his hands down her hair. He looked up at Frank who stared at him with a puzzled worried look. Kalvin pointed at Chrys. Frank, unsure of what that meant but having a sneaking suspicion tapped his back. Kal nodded. Then his ribs. Kal nodded. Hesitating tapped his chest. Kal nodded. Looking down then up Frank tapped his head. Kal shook his head no. Frank put his head in his hands.

"Sorry, to crush the moment but, I've got an announcement." Chrys said turning to the little faces shinning with love. The look on their faces was so young and innocent. So wanting of approval and love.

"Chrys, what's wrong?" Marianne asked seeing the look on her face.

Chrys breathed deep, cleared her throat and whispered, "I'm leaving."

"Where are you going?" Marybeth asked.

"To..." her breath was shallow.

"Chrys, you okay?" Kal asked hand on her shoulder. She shook her head yes. The memory of the first time she told her sisters she was dying flashed into her head. They were confused and so young. They cried and begged her not to leave them. The first time she told Frank he lost all the color in his face. He wouldn't believe her. Whispered some nonsense about it supposed to be him. She never did anything he did. She knew about the drugs and she knew his big secret. She knew he didn't stop when he said he did, so she knew what he meant. But, it wasn't true still. And Kalvin, Kalvin stood shocked. She knew how he felt, well she knew how she felt and how she hoped he felt. When the shock past the anger came. Not toward her just in general. He stood for a moment the rage boiling eventually he punched a hole in the wall.

Coming back, she finished not looking at the little eyes before her. "Heaven"

"No, silly," Sammy spoke up "Dead people are in heaven."

"Sammy, honey, I'm sick. I've been sick. Very sick for very long time. And now I'm so sick I'm going to go to heaven. With the dead people" Chrys told her her hands on the little girls' arms.

"You-you're leaving? You can't leave" Sammy's eyes poured tears out. Whimpering she ran from the room dragging Jennie with her.

"She thought I was going to save her didn't she?" Chrys asked and the twins both crying nodded. In truth, she would have. She would have gone home and found some way for them to stay with her. Whether it be by having her parents adopt them or doing it herself.

"Guys come on we knew this day would come. We talked about this. Please don't cry. Don't make this harder than it needs to be" she continued.

Glancing around the room, she knew that it wouldn't be easy. The twins were crying. Sammy and Jennie we in an adjoining room and Chrys could hear the faint child like cry. Frank stood in the corner his fist clenched and pressed against his jaw to prevent him from crying and Kalvin. Kalvin completely lost it worse than any other time she could remember. His chest was exploding with rapid breath his deep gray eyes shone bright. She couldn't help but hear the echoing of his words *"My angel my precious angel"* repeat in her mind.

"Kal" she began and he just shook his head and walked out. She didn't understand he knew about the other bruises. He knew what they meant. Looking at Frank, she couldn't deal with this. She had her pills but she was still getting sick. Kalvin had even been making her take this weird berries crushed up in spiky blue-ish leaves smothered in some weird greenish mixture. He didn't even know why he just thought it looked medicinal.

Frank taking Chrys into his arms whispered, "He loves you more than anything and he can't deal with it like you do."

Through her tears, she whispered, "He called me his angle. *Angle.*"

"I know, I know." Frank said softly.

Chrys looking up at him whispered, "I'm not okay with it any more. Dying. I'm not okay with it. I have a lot to do I've decided."

Frank just nodded and held her as she cried. He wanted so bad to tell her that it would all be okay but he couldn't. It was coming it was inevitable. He knew it, she knew it they all knew it. He wanted to tell her that Kalvin would be okay in the end but he couldn't because he wasn't so sure that it was true.

Kalvin sat outside leaning against a tree. He tried all he could to compose himself and go back, but when she came down the ladder, it was too much. He sobbed fighting the tears. He couldn't handle it. He just couldn't he slid to the ground fighting his tears as she wrapped her arms around him.

"Kal" she began and he shook his head. She knew it was too soon. He needed time so they sat there rocking as he turned and brought her close to him. Holding her close set off a whole new feeling of dread within him. Thinking that he might soon lose that after he only truly gained it so soon. He composed himself soon enough.

"Chrys" he began slowly chocking on his own words. "I-I... I love you." It was all he could manage. She sat silent waiting to see if it was okay to respond.

" I love you. That will never change. But, I'm tired of fighting. Either I win soon or don't know what to do."

"Life is a fight. I know you'll say that but maybe it is for you but not for me."

"Chrys it's your life. It's whatever you want."

"I won't stop fighting at this point for all of us but I'm just not sure how much longer I can."

"I'm sorry I've made this about me when it clearly wasn't. I love you. I will *always* love you no matter what." He smiled "My wife."

"I wish to be buried "she talked slowly gauging his reaction. It was normal: tensed shoulders, clenched fists and a pale face. "As Chrystal "Chrys" Marks Vance, please."

"Of course." He whispered half smiling. It felt wrong that he was half-happy that she wanted his name. He felt sick that he could even feel anything but pain at that. It was clear to everyone that he would never love again. The disgust he looked at Lela with proved it. On the surface, it may have seemed it was because of the way she treated Sammy and Jennie and partly it was. But, mostly he felt sick that she would live a long happy life and Chrys wouldn't. The way she tried to flirt with him his only thought was *'If she were a guy, I'd punch her.'*

His face looked twisted as they sat there. Chrys just stared at him but his eyes looked distant and lost.

"Kal? Kalvin?" Chrys whispered softly placing her hand on his shoulder.

"Huh?" he asked jumping slightly coming back. "Oh, sorry."

"It's okay to feel something other than pain and sadness." She said gently, smiling "I do."

"It's not that." he half lied.

"Then what?" she sensitively inviting him to tell. She knew he was in a delicate spot.

"I- it's- I feel like crap." He told her looking away.

"Why do you feel that way?" she asked affectionately hugging his arm.

"Other, than the obvious. Because I felt kinda happy when you wanted my name on your-"

"Oh, Kal! You shouldn't feel bad for feeling happy. I feel happy all the time." She said flipping around to face him and adoringly running her hand through his hair.

"How?" he asked his voice deep but breaking.

She smiled and leaned her forehead against him knowing the answer for the most part would hurt him more.

"I don't let the future worry me. Live for the here and now." She said pointing to both their hearts. He sighed and leaned his head on her. He didn't want to move but he knew they had to go back eventually.

They made their way up to the hut. The twins stared at them. Finally, Marianne couldn't take it and ran over to her. Holding her little sister, close Chrys almost unconsciously began talking. It seemed normal at first but slowly turned to a simple prayer.

"Please Heavenly Father hear us now. Please watch over these young people. Please send them help and grant them an escape from this island hear their prayers. Please send them strength in their time of need. In Jesus name Amen."

The day went by in a comforting soft of lull. Tears dried and little red eyes finally closed.

"We need to talk." Chrys told Frank as soon as Kalvin fell asleep. She had sat in his room with him until he couldn't force his eyes open any longer.

He sighed and replied, "I know."

She sat near him a he prodded the fire with a stick.

"I'm confused." She began "I have the bruises but none of the other symptoms. I-I just don't get it. I should be very weak and-and I'm not I should be coughing and puking. I should be very afraid but suddenly I'm not."

"What's different this time?" he asked "Other than the obvious."

"Well, clearly the island. Um, Sammy and Jennie. Oh! I almost forgot. There's that weird mixture that Kal makes me take every day." Suddenly a thought came over the dying girl.

"We need to get in to that boat, now!" she sprang up and ran for the door pausing to find him grabbing one of their weapons. She raised a questioning eyebrow and he laughed.

"It's for show." And Chrys nodded. They hastened to the boat stopping to let the the horse and wolf out to pasture. The wolf ran alongside the horse. He was tame but only came for Chrys. It was as if he could sense she was the one who healed him so he protected her. They arrived at the boat hoping the girl was sleeping or away. Sneaking in they made their way to the captains quarters searching for a radio they found a very old one, probably unused for many years.

Pushing the button Chrys prayed for an answer, a dial tone, something. But nothing.

Frank took off the dash and tried to work with the wire. In the mean time, Chrys went exploring.

Walking through the small halls Chrys tried not to made noise or attract attention. Peaking in and out of rooms Chrys came upon a newspaper from the day before the boat crash. Picking it up and beginning to read Chrys nearly fainted.

"*Ohmigod!!*" running back to where Frank was Chrys nearly screamed

"What?!" Frank asked as she thrust the newspaper in his hand.

"Look! She exclaimed as he read the title

5 Children Lost In Caribbean

Reading it further they discovered that the pilots had reported them missing when they realized their miscalculation and couldn't get back to them." An extensive search was under way." Read one of the lines

"*Ohmigod!*" Chrys squealed "They're looking for us!"

"Yeah, but we're not in the Caribbean." Frank reminded her

"Oh, yeah. But we don't know how close we are to the Caribbean." Chrys told him

"True. But, still we need to make this radio work." He said resuming his work. Eventually he got the wired so a slight static sound came over the radio.

"Frank! You did it! Okay, now let's try and find a signal..." Chrys fussed with the dial until the static stopped.

"Shit!" she said under her breath. Then thinking for a moment decided to try it.

"Hello? Can anyone hear me? Hello?" Chrys waited and nothing happened. "We are trapped on this island! Please, my name is Chrys Marks! Pleeease!" she waited again and nothing.

"Well, we tried. Better, get out of here before she comes back. I take it you're not her favorite person." Frank said trying to make her feel better as they headed toward the door. But just before they did static came on the radio.

"Did you hear that?" Chrys asked running back in

"No, what was it?" Frank asked following

"The radio!" she picked it up and listened

"Chrys Marks do you copy? This is Captain Vincent Astrvski. I repeat do you copy?!"

"I copy!" Chrys nearly shouted into the radio

"Do you know your location?" Vincent Astrvski asked

"Um, no. Not really. We were supposed to go to the Caribbean but we ended up here." Chrys told him" Please help us!"

"Stay calm. Tell me who is there with you?"

"Um, my sisters, my boyfriend and my best friend. Oh! Names. Marianne and Marybeth Marks, Kalvin Vance and Frank Stevenson."

"Okay, now stay with me. I'm going to have the FBI track this signal, okay. Now, can you tell me about the 5 of you? Is there someone I should call?"

"Um, well Mr. and Mrs. Harman and Coleen Stevenson. Also, Mr. and Mrs. Gerald and Talia Marks and Miss Kameron Vance. Please and thank you."

"Okay, I'm going to go now. But, don't worry we're coming for you, okay."

"Okay."

They exited then and just as they entered into the woods Lela came out.

"I wonder what she was doing?" Chrys asked

"I don't know. It doesn't matter. Who is Kameron Vance? Kal's mom is Wendi." Frank asked they headed up the slight hill to the waterfall. On one side, there was a mountain slope. On the other, there was a set of small hills.

"Oh, I forgot the only one he told was me. Anyway, it doesn't matter now. She's his twin sister. She was paralyzed somehow in an accident...involving Kal's gang. They haven't spoken since. So I figured they would make up this way." Chrys told him as they walked closer to the hut.

"That's insane. The last person he's going to want to see would be her. I mean especially if they...get her too late." Frank laughed softly. A sad laugh of regret and sorrow. The kind of laugh you do to avoid sadness.

"Well, he needs somebody!" Chrys protested "If we aren't found soon you'll be the only one who doesn't."

"What do you mean?" he asked helping her up the ladder.

"I meant that you have a family and other friends. You have somewhere to go where people who love."

"Seriously? You're my best friend. I have no friends like you." He told her "You're like my sister. I don't know what I'll do. But I can promise that no matter what I'll be there for them. Even Kal. Cause I know that's what you'd want."

"It's funny. Being the walking dead is well different than I imagined it." She commented while starting their breakfast. They had spent the good part of the night and next morning in the boat.

"Hey." Kal said walking from his room red-eyes.

"You sleep much?" Chrys asked

He shook his head no "You?"

"No. But you will never guess what we did!" she bounced up from the fire and wrapped her arms around his neck "We found help!"

"What?" he asked his face lighting up "Where? How?"

"We went to the boat and found an old radio and Frank made it work. But, I found this paper." She said handing him the paper. He scanned it and nodded

"But how does this help?"

"Well, then I talked on the radio to a Captain Vincent Astrvski and he said he would call the FBI and they would track the signal and find us!" she gleamed and knew in his mind he only thought of her.

"You are amazing!" he said kissing her as the baby cried. He laughed.

"What?" she asked carrying her out.

"Nothin." He laughed shifting the food it was an odd but almost wonderful sight. A couple so in love but separated by the promise of death yet united by the call of innocence and youth. It wasn't hard for him to love her but he couldn't love the kiss death bestowed her.

She looked at him as Jennie crawled over into his lap. A sudden look of fear and confusion passed over him. She laughed to herself thinking: *It's okay. You don't need to know what to do.* The twins came out now asking

"Where's Frank?"

"Out getting meat." Chrys said

"Oh," Marybeth said nonchalantly turning to Marianne "That's probably where Sammy is."

"What?" Chrys asked her mind flicking to Lela running from the woods.

"We heard a noise and then footsteps but I guess it was you guys" Marianne told her

"How long ago was this?" Kal asked

"I dunno 45 minutes, maybe. Why?" Beth said

"*Shit*" Kal said as Chrys related the mornings happenings including seeing Lela

They headed for the door commanding the twins finish breakfast and tell Frank what happened. They searched everywhere Sammy would know and nothing. Running into the woods they called for her and yet nothing.

"Sammy! Sammy!!" Chrys screamed running through the woods. Into parts uncharted. Kal running behind her grabbed her arm holding her back. Tears streaming from her eyes she struggled momentarily before falling into his arms.

"She wouldn't come here. She doesn't know it any better than we do." He told her running his hand down her hair "We're gonna find her. It'll be okay. We're gonna go back to the US and then they will have a happy life with us."

She sniffed "Us?"

"Us." He stated simply "they're too young to be your siblings." He lied he knew perfectly well that they weren't yet he said it anyway "And you're probably going to end up raising them anyway. So, I figured why not make them ours?"

She stared at him with blank amazement. *Ours.* It wasn't something she had hope left for, having children. She figured she would die young and Kalvin, she feared for him. She prayed the streets wouldn't be where he ended up again. But, with children...

"Come on." He said. A new faith that she would live rising within him. "Let's look near where you saw Lela."

"Okay." She said walking with her arms wrapped around him.

They searched and searched for an hour or so. Chrys nearly giving up hope when she heard a slight muffled call.

"Kal!" Chrys said softly. He patted her hand as they slowly made their way toward the sound. They ended up outside the boat. Chrys fumed with anger. Lela had to be behind this where else could Sammy have gone. Quietly they made their way to the boat. They snuck in the way Frank and Chrys had earlier and met Frank inside.

"Frank?" Chrys asked confused at the scene before her. Kalvin stared at him, catching his eye Frank shook his head.

"Chrys! Hey, the twins told me what happened and I knew she was to blame so I came over here. I didn't figure id' beat you." He explained calmly. The measurement the girl had once held over him fell to pieces when Chrys got hurt. She was forever more important.

"Oh, well where's Sammy?" Chrys asked softly

"She won't say." Frank said

"I will *not* leave without her and neither will she." Chrys stamped her foot to add a dramatic flair. She ran down the halls and in and out of rooms. The whole time the girl screamed and had to be held back. Climbing to the upper deck Chrys spotted the little figure. She was bound and gagged under a tarp. The little girl squirmed and let out muffled screams until she saw it was Chrys.

She threw her arms around Chrys's shoulders and she carried her back down.

"That is it!" Chrys said "I am through with your crap! Fix the boat and send her away." Chrys walked out and shock and happiness went over Lela's face.

"Never." Kal said sternly "That will never happen. You're comin with us." He grabbed her arm and dragged her back. He locked her in the animals stall and ordered the wolf to guard her.

He explained that he and Frank were going to fix the boat so they could find out their location. Also, to try and locate 'that Vincent guy.'

Chrys waited until they were gone to sneak down to the barn. She ordered the wolf to do the same before walking to Lela's stall.

Letting the others out to pasture she waited.

"What?" the girl snapped

"Why are you here?" she asked harshly when Chrys didn't answer

"To make a deal with the devil." She stated

Lela raised her eyebrows "What kind of deal?"

"You tell them I went to look for supplies or something. And their home free when the plane comes. And you get to go on that plane." Chrys said softly

"So you just want me to lie to your boyfriend so you what? Get to stay here?"

"Die." Chrys corrected "Die here. Leukemia- it's a killer."

The girl nodded "Doesn't seem I have a choice."

"No, you really don't." Chrys said sticking her hand in the stall "Deal?"

The girl smiled a wicked smile "Deal."

Chrys wrote a note that night and gently laid in near the fire pit.

Dear Family,

Please accept my decision. There is no use in pretending I'll be okay. Please just go home. Oh, and take the girl, too. I'm sorry.

Love,

Chrystal Vance

Kal picked up the note as he walked in calling "Chrys? We got the boat to turn on, but the holes still there. I don't think we can fix it." He opened the note and dropped to the floor.

"Frank!" he yelled and the boy ran in picking up the note. Kalvin who had rested where he fell stood then heading for the door. Frank close behind. Running into the barn, he shoved the note at the girl who merely replied

"Told me she was going to get something."

"What?" Kal asked teeth clenched

She shrugged and Kal punched through the wall next to her.

"What?"

"She- she didn't say!" Lela exclaimed backing further into her stall. "Really!"

"You're lying! Tell me where she went!" Kalvin was screaming his fist inches from her every time he thrusted his hand through the wall.

"I'm not!" she repeated but it wasn't good enough he didn't believe her. Truthfully, she was lying but she was supposed to.

"Kal. Kal she doesn't know!" Frank said pulling him back

"Yes, she does!" Kalvin exclaimed pulling away. His fist connecting with Frank's face. Only then did he stop.

"Dude, I- I'm-" Kal stammered stepping back as Frank pulled himself up off the ground.

"I know." He said running his hand over eye and upper cheek. They left then Lela staring scared and shocked.

"We have to find her." Kal said as a light rain came down

"She doesn't want to be found. And there's so much forest here. I-I don't know if we will." Frank told him as they stared out from the waterfall.

"*We have to*" Kalvin whispered. He looked over at Frank who's eye and cheek were turning black and blue.

"Punch me." He said locking his hands behind his back. "Come on do it. Punch me."

"I'm not going to punch you cause you want me to. That's insane!"

"Frank, punch me. Do it. I lost my temper and nearly smashed that girl in the face! *Punch me.*"

"Oh, that's what this is about. Dude, seriously you'd never do that to Chrys. Hell, you can't even get mad at her."

"I don't know that." Kal looked off into space thinking. *I never changed. I'm the same old gang bangin asshole.*

****

Chrys walked silently imagining the scene that was set to unfold when her note was discovered. Silently she walked through uncharted territory. Confused and a tad sad. *Why? Why do I have to do this? I want to be with him. Damn, I hate to hurt them but either way I would have.* She cursed the say she was born. Cursed God's very existence. *I get it, okay. I get what it's like to lose everything you love. I know I'm blessed. I know so please stop. I'm privileged, I've always known that and he's a good man. Really he is. I don't know what more you want from me.* She pleased with God to end it. She didn't have anything in particular in mind. Death or a cure. It just needed to be over.

She walked for hours before dark fell and she couldn't walk anymore. Slowly she fell asleep and dreamt that the plane came then and no one looked for her no one cared. She woke up in a cold sweat the dead of night surrounding her and she ran. She ran until she couldn't run anymore and she collapsed. Her hand under her head and she felt the bruise. And she cried. She cried knowing that is where she would die. In a bed of leave lost in a forest on an undiscovered island- alone. She did this to herself she knew

84

that. She knew she could got back but she didn't have the energy. She laid there starring at the ground beside her. Once again letting sleep carry her far away.

****

Telling the girls was harder than either boy imagined. Marybeth screamed that she hated Chrys and Marianne backhanded her. The scene was full of tears and angry-hatred. Kalvin slipped outside and Marianne followed him.

"Kalvin?" she said softly and weakly he smiled in response "Why did she do this?"

"She doesn't want us to go through it again." He whispered softly.

"But- but the plane?" the little girl asked.

"I don't know." He couldn't look at her just held his arm out. Slipping closer to him, she whispered.

"She still loves you." He just squeezed her shoulder while she leaned her head against his waist.

"Marianne" he began , she nodded "I'll find her, okay? Everything will be okay."

"Do you believe that?" she asked.

"I have to." He answered.

She nodded as Marybeth came out. She walked over and took Kal's hand. He smiled and let her stand there with him. Eventually he led them inside and sat there around the fire. They all did even Sammy

"I'm not a bad guy." Kal said "I just did some bad things."

Frank smiled "We all have." Glancing at the young girls sitting near them and laughed sadly "Or will."

"I'm going to bed." He added a few minutes later.

"K." Kalvin said.

"We know." Marianne said after a few minutes "that- that you're not a bad guy.'

85

"But," Marybeth spoke up "What's going to happen if we don't find her. Or-or if she dies?"

"What do you mean?" he asked. No matter how many times the scene played where they cried over Chrys it never seemed to get easier. Only harder.

"Are you gonna go away?" Marianne asked

"No," he told her "I don't have anywhere else to go. Look, I'm big and scary I get it but this- the 7 of us- is all I got."

"Plus, I promised I wouldn't let them go back to where ever they're from." He said motioning to Sammy. Sammy's eyes shot up and a slight smile peered out.

"Really?" she asked

"Mhmm." He smiled as she walked over to him sat in his lap and wrapped her arms around him. He didn't know what to do, but he didn't need to. He already was doing the right thing. She laid there, he laid his hand on her back, and she smiled.

"But what about us?" Marybeth asked. Kal smiled and patter her knee unsure of what to say. He didn't need to, she knew he would do whatever he thought Chrys would. It was a long night for all in the little hut.

****

It shocked her that she woke up the next morning. She expected to end up in the kingdom beyond. Yet, she woke up, sitting near her- she ever more shocked to see was Lela. Waiting there for hours. Both girls jumped

"How did you- what are- why?" Chrys stuttered.

"They miss you." Lela stated "So, I came to find you." She was half telling the truth. Partly she was there for that reason and partly it was because she was afraid that Kalvin would come back.

Chrys looked puzzled "But how-"

"Okay, that's not the whole truth. You're friend- the big one. He freaked when he found your note. Started punching anything. Including your littler friend. Scared me shitless. Reminded me of my daddy. I guess that partly made me realize how terrible

I've been. I know I don't have a n excuse but that was normal in my house and then the lady at the orphanage said to. So, I thought it was normal and everybody did it." She explained

"But the boat?" Chrys reminded her

"Oh, I went to talk to her but she freaked and I panicked. So I took her. Then I saw you guys leaving the boat and got scared so- you know the rest."

"But that doesn't- how did you find me?" Chrys asked standing across from her.

"Oh, I saw you leaving and then the smaller guy came down babbling something about 'he's gonna kill me but you know where she is' I assumed he meant the angry big guy. Then he looked at me and said the weirdest thing-"

"Wait what's the other part of why you realized you were wrong you never said" Chrys asked.

"This is it." Lela told her "He said 'He's not a bad guy, he just made mistakes. So that means you've done the same. Fix them and find her.' So id did. I thought you were dead do I stayed her and waited. I don't know what for."

"Oh, I never thought about what you went through. I only thought of what you were doing."

"That's how you should have. It helped me." She told her "Come on, they want you back."

"I can't. I-I can't do this to them again. They had to watch me die once before and I won't make them relive that. It was hard enough for them and I didn't even die."

"Do you wanna die?" Lela asked confused.

"I want this crap disease to either take me or leave me. Just be over with."

"That's selfish." Lela remarked handing her a piece of paper

Dear Chrys,

Please come back. We need you dying or not. Please.

"I can't though. I'm sick of hurting people."

"You don't hurt them unless you're not there. They want you there no matter if you're sick. You're not out here for them. You're here for you, because you want to die alone. You're so afraid that you think running will fix that. Well, trust me it won't."

"And, you know what? You have people who love you and care about you and you just wanna throw that away!? That's so stupid!"

Chrys had nothing to say she just stared at the girl for a moment. Lela grabbed her until she saw them. Kal smiling at her sisters Frank holding the baby. What she didn't realize was Kalvin smiled because Frank told him Lela went to find Chrys. And he had to believe him.

"Hey fellas look who I found!" Lela called. Kalvin's eyes light up as they all raced over to her. She let them hug her but she squirmed in Lela's grasp. When Kalvin came over to her, she broke free and ran. With nowhere to go, she dove off the waterfall. She wouldn't die but Kal didn't care. He dove after her.

The water was cool but Kal splashed around until he found her. She pulled away, but he was stronger. He just held her arm as she struggled. Eventually she just stopped and starred at him. Wet and dripping he just pulled her close to him.

"Why?" he whispered "Why don't you want to be here?" He paused "With me."

She looked away. She shook her head.

"Chrys, tell me." He pleaded

"It's not that." She said "It's not that at all. I love you. More than anything. And I thought, I thought maybe if I left it would be easier for you."

He shook his head "Never."

"I know. I was just scared and I still am. But I don't- it's not. I don't' know how to be scared. It's not fair to any of us."

He hugged her as they floated there. He laughed "You can be scared. We all are. 'Fear is not the absence of courage just the presence of humanity.' Someone once told me that."

"That's smart" Chrys laughed. She knew who said that and sometimes she forgot the things she said.

"See?" he said pushing her hair away "We need you. I need you."

She smiled and laid her head on his chest as he pulled them to shore. They laid there for a moment before Chrys began to cry. Kalvin reached over and held her close to him stroking her hair.

Frank came down the bank and placed a hand on her shoulder. She lifted her head and smiled.

"I'm sorry." She whispered

Frank shook his head "No, don't worry."

"Chrys!" Marianne called running down to her she wrapped her arms around her sister.

"We missed you! Don't go away again, okay?" Marybeth asked kissing her sisters cheek. Chrys glanced up at Lela who stood arms folded smirking.

"Thanks" Chrys mouthed and she gave two thumbs up in response.

****

"Can you pinpoint their location Lieutenant?"

"No Captain. There doesn't seem to be anything there."

"Well, keep looking. I talked to that girl."

"Are you sure, Captain?"

"Yes, I'm sure."

"They're gonna pull us off soon, Captain."

"I don't give a damn what 'they're gonna do. We are finding those kids by order or not!"

"Okay, Captain."

"I'm tired of taking orders from a suit in an office. Those kids were scared and lost and I promised her I would find her. I'm not leaving them!"

"Okay, Captain."

The Lieutenant was a young man of only 25. A toll strong man by the name of Nicoli Astrvski, the young brother of our Captain Vincent Astrvski. Vincent was a young man of about 30 with deep eyes and dark features, and a passion for his job. He and his three brothers, once orphaned in Russia fueled his desire to love by 'no man left behind.'

His bother Nicoli did not share his passion. Left in a country dealt with blow after blow. Living in turmoil lead him to desire order and structure. But, his brother he trusted so he went forth with their mission.

Flying above the ship was a third brother. Derk Astrvski radioed down.

"Captain, do you copy?"

"I copy, Sergeant."

"I may have located the island."

"Fly ahead and radio your coordinated.

"10-4"

Derk Astrvski looked a bit liked each of his brothers. Deep eyes and dark features. At only 23, he was tall, strong, and as determined as his brothers. His determination differed from theirs, his passion was for the odd and extraordinary which is why he took to the skies.

****

The day proceeded like many others before them. A quiet simplicity Chrys grew to love. No distractions no heartache just pure quiet simplicity. Every action once over looked now treasured by all. Every smile, every laugh, every tear; treasured.

Two days passed with no sign of the plane nor a boat. All had nearly given up hope when came the roar of the jet engine. All the young people ran outside to watch the pilot search for landing space.

Hovering in mid-air Sargent Derk Astrvski radioed to his brothers.

"Found them. I repeat I *have* found them. Do you copy?"

"We copy." The boys on the boat answered "Full speed ahead, brother."

Jokingly Nicoli answered "Ay Ay, Captain." But, all joking aside the Captain and his shipmate made their way to the island with the coordinates the third brother gave them.

Seeing this all the residents of the little island made their way to the beach waving their arms above their head and shouting.

The boat pulled gently up to the shore, the young Captain hopping off and running over "Is one of you Chrystal Marks?" the word stung her. She'd forgotten she used Marks. But, Kalvin knew why or thought he did. Truthfully, he didn't care either.

"I am." She said softly glancing at the smiling Kalvin.

Kalvin only noticed the younger man eyeing his tattoos.

Kalvin laughed proclaiming "I come in peace."

This made the young man smile slightly. His face was cold and stern but you could tell he was a kind man. The helicopter above circled and Chrys suggested they go. She sent the twins back to get things and Lela too.

When they returned they were helped onto the boat. Chrys turning to their little oasis waved as she heard the moan of the wolf.

"I set them free." Beth whispered.

Chrys nodded and whispered "Good-bye." To her home.

It turned out they had been gone for many months. They whole thing was a big show. Their parents shuffled them around form one press conference to another. "Amazing" "Marvelous" "A real show stopper" Words but meaningless, Chrys ached for the simplicity. The beauty of her island hut. She may not have had treatment but she was happy most of the time. The concrete prison of the hospital left her a shell. *This* she thought *is why I nearly died the first time. Prison. Captive.* Sure, she had visitors, including the Astrvski boys but it wasn't the same. She ached for the happy days they spent there. She wanted to go back. She wanted to be there and nowhere else. She hated the hospital and everything within it.

"It smells like death." Chrys complained one Friday as she and Kalvin ate lunch in her hospital room "The whole place. Death roams the halls and waits at my door. Slowly rapping on it as I lay awake night. Waiting for the night I get up and answer it."

"You're being dramatic." Kalvin told her handing her her homework. Every day since she was admitted Frank gave Kalvin her homework and every day, he 'forgot' to give it to her until right before he left. Every day. Not today.

She looked at him "Something wrong?"

He shook his head no "I remembered today, that's all." She didn't believe him but she took them anyway and set them aside.

"Do it." He told her

"Why?" she asked pulling them back over.

"Because we're- well you'll see." He told her as she started in on math. She went through math when he suddenly stepped out of the room. She didn't really notice. She was busy. She just kept going stopping to check if he was okay. But, he wasn't out there. *He probably went to the cafeteria.* She continued on with her homework. Eventually she came across a little envelope. It was a light baby blue color with the same emblem as on her necklace and his ring. Carefully she slid her finger under the top. Gently she slid a little not out.

8 o'clock east parking lot. Formal.

"*What?*" she asked running out of the room "Kal? Kalvin!" she called down the hallway

92

"He left darling." Said one of the nurses as she passed by.

"Thank you." Chrys said darting back into her room, checking the time. It was 5 o' clock. She had two hours. She sat down and finished her homework and then re-reading the note decided she wanted to dress up. Kalvin didn't let her pay for their dates so they didn't often do anything really fancy. She smiled as one of the nurses helped her get ready. It was sad but they knew her by name. They had for a while. It was their way of making her feel comfortable. She knew they had very little hope she would get better but she never argued. She knew better, she knew they had to be pessimists. They worked in a hospital, people died every day. But, nonetheless, they curled her hair and pinned it up in a loose bun. They zipped her dress and helped her hide the bald spots. It was a side effect of the chemo. They weren't big yet and her hair was long enough to cover them. Most of the time she just wore hoodies. She refused to wear the standard bandanas that cancer patients wear.

"Thanks." She said softly as she slipped out the door in her deep blue dress. It was supposed to be her prom dress, but, for some reason she felt she should wear it that night. She didn't know why but she felt it was going to be special. Kalvin wasn't a very romantic guy, he tried but he just wasn't. She didn't mind, she didn't need flowers and random chocolates she just needed someone who didn't mind hospital rooms and endless sick days. She just needed him.

"Ooo, big date?" the receptionist named Caren asked handing her the sign out booklet.

"I think so." Chrys told her signing herself out mumbling to herself "Return time, um later." She left then walking to the east parking lot. Mostly it was deserted. The east parking lot was for patients who would check out in a few days, patients with visiting hours. They dropped enforcing them for the cancer patients a while back. Mainly they say that but really they enforce most of them but Kalvin would come in all odd hours. And Chrys befriended the nurses so she doesn't have them any longer.

"Hey," Kalvin said stepping out from the shadows.

"Oh!" Chrys jumped "Creeper! You scared the crap out of me!"

He laughed opening the door to a limo.

"Wow! What's the occasion?" Chrys asked sitting down.

"You look beautiful." He told her sliding in next to her.

She smiled "You don't look to shabby yourself." Pulling a piece of his long black hair behind his ear. He had it mostly pulled back. He wore a black tuxedo and incidentally his vest under the tuxedo was blue. He smiled

"I have to show you something." He slipped out of his tuxedo coat and his vest then opening his shirt Chrys became confused

"What are you doing?"

"Nothing bad." He said pulling his shirt off "It's okay." He turned and pointed to his shoulder blade.

"Kalvin." Chrys stated running her hands over it. Permanently etched into his back was her name in cursive surrounded faintly by that same emblem. "Oh, wow, Kalvin I-I don't know what to say."

"You don't have to." He told her slipping back into his clothes "I figured I got all these tattoos why not get one that has- I don't know meaning."

She threw her arms around him and kissed his cheek as the limo pulled up to their destination. They exited, Kalvin leading her into the restaurant. It was a nice restaurant. Not what she's used to he was sure but the smile on her face assured him she didn't care. He should know better but he began to worry more and more that she would leave him.

They were seated at a little table with candles. She smiled as they sat but she knew it wasn't going to end well when the food of the couple a few tables over came out and she felt sick.

"You don't have to eat." He said taking her hand "just don't look at it and you'll be fine."

She nodded keeping her head slightly turned left. It went fine until the waiter asked for their order racking off the names of foods.

"Maybe," Kalvin said squeezing her hand "we'd better just leave."

"I'm sorry to ruin it." She said softly as they left "I tried, I did. I wanted it to go just how you did."

He laughed, "It went perfectly. And besides it isn't over yet."

"No?" she asked holding his hand tighter "So, I guess I didn't *totally* ruin it."

"You'd never ruin it." He told her "I have a question."

"Okay." She said as they sat back down in their limo.

"Why- well why...why me?" he blurted, then realizing she didn't quite understand added "Why me and not some rich guy? Why did you pick me?"

"I could ask the same." She told him "I love you and not some rich guy. I don't care about money. I never have. I only wanted to help make up for what you were cheated of. I never meant to make you feel inadequate. Because you're not. You are the best thing that ever happened to me."

"No I'm not." He said his head down and she nodded smiling

"Yes, you are. You can say you're not but that doesn't make it true because it's not. I love you, isn't that enough?"

"Of course but-"he just stopped talking and sighed

"I know you've been trying to be perfect. I could tell but I don't need perfect. I fell in love with the guy fresh off the street unsure of what to do. The real guy and I just want him back." She told him scotching closer and taking his hand back. He sighed and nodded

"I should've known that. But, it makes the rest of the date more...me." He laughed and she leaned against him.

"Good. It's about time we do something normal." She smiled and laughed "Right?"

"Maybe." He teased. Eventually they stopped and Kalvin told her

"Close your eyes." She did and he led her up what seemed like a few steps. When she opened her eyes, she laughed. It almost took her breath away. It wasn't beautiful and it wasn't very romantic but what it meant was so much more than that. She was staring at the street where she first met Kalvin. She stepped down off the little stoop she was on and began to walk.

"Oh, Kal." She said softly as he ran down behind her.

He grabbed her arm and pulled her back. She turned to him startled. "Come back." He pulled her onto the stoop again. "It's dangerous." He told her letting her arm go. She smiled and took his hand again. Leaning over the railing to look. She sighed contented.

"Oh, Kal." She said again. It wasn't that the place was beautiful under moonlight or even in the daylight but it was so special to her. It was special that he remembered the exact spot and it was special that he brought her there.

"Kal, this is wonderful." She laughed, "Even if it's scary."

"Yea, sorry if I thought you were gonna be scared I would've brought the gun. But, I know that, that scares you too, so." He said nervously squeezing her hand.

"No, no, it's fine. It's perfect." She said leaning her head back onto his arm. She stared for a minute before the fireworks went off. She jumped and screamed a little, placing her hand on her heart.

"Sorry." He said sheepishly

"No, it's pretty. Did you do this?" she asked smiling.

"Yeah. Just wait it gets better." He told her slipping his hands around her waist and resting his head on her shoulders. He kissed her neck and she smiled.

"Okay, ready?" he asked slipping down off the steps.

"Wait! It's not safe! Kalvin, wait!" she hissed stepping closer.

He smiled and put his finger to his lips "Shh." And she nodded quieting down. Hearts started exploding into the sky. He took her hand and bent down on one knee. She gasped.

"Kal." She whispered. He smiled and slipped a ring onto her finger. She was shaking and she just let the tears flow. He looked up into the sky so she followed his gaze. As a K and a C lit up the sky, he asked her

"Chrys, will you marry me?"

Shaking and crying she hopped off of the steps and threw herself into his arms.

"Yes." She said smiling as he wiped away her tears "Of course." He picked her up off her feet as he encased her in his arms. He kissed her and then let her down.

"Get in the limo, *now.*" He told her and she looked around.

"Kalvin, what's wrong?" she asked stepping fearfully closer to him.

"Nothing...yet." He told her pointing to the limo "Go, Chrys."

She ran to the limo slipping in she rolled down the window and watched as he walked slowly around alley.

"Kal!" she called out and he whipped around as she was waving to come back. He held up his finger to say 1 minute. She nodded and sat watching him nervously. After a few minutes, he came back and simply stated.

"It was nothing."

"Then why did you go?"

"I thought I heard something, guess I was paranoid." He told her plainly.

"You weren't scared?" she asked laughed, "No, duh, that was a dumb question."

"Only, for you." He told her. He had to take her back to the hospital now and endure the joyful screaming of the nurses and receptionist she befriended. He smiled, he didn't mind as much as it seemed like he did. They arrived and walked back into the hospital he stood off to the side as the nurses walked over to her. The receptionist Caren and the nurse who helped her dress, Maryse, along with another nurse, Belinda. It was late and there wasn't much happening so they could talk. Kalvin was standing a bit behind them as Chrys told them what happened, hands in his pockets eyes down. He wasn't good in these kind of situations. He knew when she told them the news. She held her hand out and the others girls' eyes went wide. They looked over at him and he waved smiling sheepishly. They laughed and Chrys pulled him over.

Whispering "Get used to it. We still have people to tell." He nodded nervously.

"What's wrong?" she asked as the girls said things and hugged him. He whispered back

"Tell you later." And then she nodded. The girls said they were going to throw her a hospital party. That's what they called any happenings that went on there.

"Thank you, girls, really." Chrys said as they walked toward their room.

"Behave, children, I've got to come give you your shot soon." Belinda said jokingly winking.

"Okay, Lindy." Chrys laughed. "Oh, she's crazy."

He nodded "Chrys?"

"Yeah?" she asked leaning her head on his arm

"Do I have to be here when you tell your parents?" he asked looking away.

"Um, why?" she asked as they entered her room.

"They already don't like me and tacking on I'm a 19 year old former gang member who is marrying your 17 year old daughter doesn't sound like something they'll like." He said looking down.

She rubbed his arm, "No, you don't have to."

"Thanks." He said as they sat down.

"Now, I get to drag you through wedding planning! And Frank too." She laughed "Mainly because all my friends are guys, children or nurses."

He smiled, and they turned on the TV. He fell asleep in the chair by the time Belinda came in. She gave Chrys her shot and then sat next to her commenting

"I guess I didn't have to worry." Chrys smiled, slightly. The shot made her feel dizzy and nauseous at first.

"Lindy?" she asked after a moment.

"Yes, sweetheart?" Belinda was a kind middle-aged woman, approximately 47, of Hispanic origin. She was of moderate stature with dark eyes and long dark hair. While Maryse was a young woman, about 24, fresh out of nursing school. She was of African American origin. She had braided hair she kept up constantly and bright eyes. Her laugh was contagious and she instantly liked Chrys. Caren was a woman of about 30, but she had wisdom beyond her years. She was of Caucasian and Asian origin. She had long black hair and bright blue eyes. She liked Chrys because she was one of the only patients who constantly thanked her, and helped out when she could. She didn't complain about her illness just asked about Caren's son. He was 5 years old and had cancer like Chrys did. He would come in and spend days with Chrys laughing and dancing around. Caren smiled when she saw the look Chrys had every time she saw the little boy. He called her "Auntie Chrys."

"Well, do you think that- I don't know. Why is he asking me to marry him?"

"Oh, sweetheart!" Belinda laughed "He loves you that is *so* obvious. Some people believe you're too young but I think that true love can come at any age. He just doesn't know how to handle love. That's all. He's confused and scared and he's not used to that. Where he comes from, love isn't common. Death is, love not so much. Darling he loves you and doesn't know how to show it."

"Yeah?" Chrys asked looking over at him sleeping in the chair.

"Would he spend days here if he didn't?" Belinda asked walking over to him, "Pretend to sleep and I'll show you."

"Okay?" Chrys said skeptically laying down closing her eyes.

"Hey, kid wake up. Kalvin." Belinda said tapping his shoulder. He jerked awake by habit grabbing at his side, for his gun.

"None of that boy." Belinda told him.

"I don't carry it anymore. It scares her." Kalvin said motioning to Chrys.

"Mhmm." Belinda nodded "She's worried you know. That you're only marrying her because you think you should."

"What?!" he exclaimed, sitting straight up.

"Yea, it's not true is it?" Belinda asked slyly picking up some of Caren's sons' things.

"No! That's crazy!" he said, becoming really quiet. Then asking softly "Can I ask you something?"

"Sure, thing hon'." Belinda told him sitting next to him.

"How do I? I don't know- how do I do this love thing?" Kalvin asked nervously shifting.

"Just be yourself, that's who she loves. Not some perfect guy. She understands where your from isn't where she was- it just isn't. But she don't care. Just love her and tell her that, she doesn't want more." Belinda told him and he nodded smiling. He was nervous still but only a little. Belinda left then and Kalvin walked over to Chrys's bed. Sliding in slightly.

"Chrys." He whispered shaking her lightly.

"Hmm?" She asked sitting up.

He slid in next to her, kissing her softly he whispered

"I love you, you know that right?"

"Of course I do. You know I love you, right?" she asked "With all my heart?"

He slipped his hands around her waist kissing her cheek he repeated "With all my heart."

She snuggled in close to him, burying her head into his chest. She pulled the blanket over them and she snuggled in closer.

"Stay tonight, please?" she asked gently. And he nodded tuning over to face her, arms still around her.

They slept like that until Maryse came in in the morning.

"Chrys, Chrys!" she whispered "Wake up! Your family is here!"

Kalvin shot up nearly throwing himself from the bed. Scrambling to make it look like he hadn't been there all night. This caused Chrys to wake up, letting out a light scream. Chrys still in her dress and Kalvin in his tuxedo they hurried to find clothes for him while she dressed down. When it looked like he just came early, Maryse let in her family, administering her shots.

"Hey, darling." Her father said and Chrys rolled her eyes. Kalvin stood up so, her mom could sit.

"How are you?" her mother asked forcing herself not to look uncomfortable there and trying not to look over at Kalvin.

"Fine. I have cancer, you know." Chrys said sharply. She hated it when they pretended they cared. If it were up to them, they wouldn't have kids. Their jobs and each other are all they cared about, according to Chrys. Her and the twins were a political move. The twins came in then and she hugged them and they stood over near Kalvin.

"Hi." Marybeth said to him

"Hey." He told her noticing a slight cut above her eye. "Marianne punch you again?" he teased

"What? Oh, no. I fell." She told him blushing.

He nodded suspicious. "Someone else hit you?" he asked and she looked away.

"Marybeth, who?" he asked. He might have been harsh on her but she was Chrys's sister and she would die if anything happened to her baby sisters.

Marybeth walked away then and Marianne whispered "Dad." Kalvin didn't look at first but she tapped him and pointed to her father "Dad did."

Kalvin looked from her to Marybeth to her father, catching Marybeth's eye she nodded looking scared.

"He was mad because we got off the island. And Marybeth told him he was an asshole." She said the last word softly, the way little kids did when they weren't sure if they should. "Then she said that she wished he would die so Chrys didn't have to. That it was all his fault and she wished she had a different dad. They were all screaming and I missed something then he backhanded her. But, don't do anything, okay? Not now." She said pulling at his arm as he started to walk over.

"After" he said "After the news."

"News?" Marianne asked "What news?"

"Okay, everyone I have some news- well we do." Chrys said looking over at him, this was his chance to leave but he was pissed now and he wasn't going anywhere.

"Well," she said standing up near him. He was now over near her bed. "We're engaged!"

"*Ohmigosh*!" the twins squealed hugging them.

Her parents just stared at them. Her mother looked faint and her father was shocked and then angry. He screamed about how Kalvin was no good, you're too young, and he won't allow it. They just listened to him rant about Kalvin and Chrys's disease and her age and blah blah blah. When he was done, Kalvin spoke up

"Done?" he asked and just kept going "I don't think you have any room to talk. I don't just have kids to have them. My life isn't about myself. Yea, I screwed up. So what? Get over it. I don't hit my kids, you asshole!" Kalvin yelled getting very close to his face.

"What?" Chrys asked, "Kal, he doesn't hit us."

"Ask Marybeth that. Or better yet Marianne, Marybeth is too scared to say anything." Kalvin told her still inches from her father.

"What? Bethy is that true?" Chrys asked holding onto Marybeth's hand. She was young no matter what she had gone through, she was only 11 and she was scared. She nodded stepping back as her father attempted to step toward her. In a split second, Kalvin had him by the shirt against the wall.

"*Don't even think of it.*" Kalvin said teeth clenched. Chrys told the twins to get onto her bed and close their eyes.

"Kal, take-take him outside." Chrys said and he looked back confused. "Please?"

So, he did. He dragged him outside shoving him. He looked furious and if you didn't know him, you would be scared. His muscles tightened and flexed with every movement, his eyes cold, his mouth in a tight line. Chrys leading the way shoved the doors open; furiously she stopped dead in her tracks. Swinging around to face her father who struggled in Kalvin's grip.

"Don't bother." She hissed, "He's stronger than you." Her father stopped momentarily. "I ought to let him beat you to a pulp. I ought to, but I won't because I'm better than you are, we both are. How dare you hit her, you spineless bastard."

She paused and then said, "Let him go" so calmly it shocked everyone. Kalvin let her father go and stepped behind her.

"Chrys," he whispered, "*Why* did you do that?"

"No, you stay right here!" she told her father stepping closer Kalvin close behind. "I'm so damn tired of you. I'm not a political statement I'm a person. My cancer isn't a political statement it's a disease that is *killing* me! I'm so tired of you just having us around to look good. Either you shape up and act like a real father or just get the hell out of my life! I will not let you hurt them! And you know what? Kalvin is twice the man you'll ever even pretend to be. So, get lost."

"You, little *bitch*." He hissed slapping her across the face.

"Bastard!" Kalvin grabbed him by the shoulders and threw him to the ground. Chrys turned her head until he was done. He left her father battered and bruised. He had broken ribs and possibly a broken arm. Chrys's mother dragged him away and Chrys walked over to Kalvin. He stood staring

"I'm sorry. I-I he hit her and then he hit you and-and I'm not always here and-" he stopped and looked at her. She wasn't angry. He got it then. She had him let her father go so he would do something. She wanted Kalvin to do that. He smiled and finished his sentence calmly. "It could have been you."

She smiled and took his hand, her engagement ring cold against his palm. He looked over when she stopped. There was blood dripping from her nose. She tipped her head back pinching her nose.

"Sorry, side effect, I guess." Chrys mumbled he laughed. "What?"

"Your voice." He told her "with your nose plugged up it sounds funny."

She smiled and they walked in.

"Oh, Chrys, what happened?" Caren asked running out from behind the desk.

"Nose bleed, no biggie." Chrys said waving it off.

"No, no you haven't had your chemo today, you shouldn't do that." Caren said leading her over to a chair "Wait here I'll get Belinda."

"I'm fine, she's just worried. But, there's no need." Chrys said seeing the look on Kalvin's face.

The twins came out of the children's area then. Where they housed the sick young children. They smiled and held Caren's little boy, Eric, by the hand.

"Eric!" Chrys exclaimed waving

"Auntie Chrys!" he said running over to her, hopping up into her lap. She squeezed him and he poked her shoulder.

"Yes?" she asked as he snuggled back further.

"You nose is bleedin."

"I know, honey. It's nothing."

He nodded "Happen to me." He told her poking her again.

"Auntie Chrys, there's a big scary man." He whispered.

She laughed "Honey, that's Kalvin. He's not scary. He's just big. Say hi."

He hopped up and walked over to Kalvin looking down.

"Hey buddy." Kalvin said bending down in front of Eric. Eric smiled then and took Kalvin's hand.

"Come here." He said taking Kalvin to his mother's desk. "Look, it's you!" he pointed to a picture on her desk. There sat a picture of Chrys, Kalvin, Frank and the three hospital workers she had befriended. Next to it was a picture of Caren, Eric and her husband and one of Eric and Chrys. Chrys laughed while Eric took Kalvin all around.

"Chrys, he's not gonna die is he?" Marianne asked watching them.

Chrys sighed "I don't know, Annie, I don't know."

They sat silently for a moment before Marybeth spoke up.

"Why did you pick him to marry?"

"I love, him Marybeth. What more does anyone need?" Chrys snapped frustrated that everyone seemed to ask that.

"He's just so...rough." She told her sister "And- and unstable."

"Unstable?" Chrys asked

"You saw what he did out there. He's got blood on his shirt, Chrysie!" Marybeth protested

"You watched that?" Chrys asked "Look he was only protecting us. Us and Frank are the only people he has and he can't lose that. So he protects us like he did out there. He's not going to hit *us*, don't worry."

"I know that. That's not what I meant." Marybeth told her, "I meant that if-if you...well then he would go bonkers."

"First off, I'm going to be fine. And second, he's handling it better now. It's a learned process that he's never had to learn before. When bad things happened he shot them or ran." Chrys told her "But, I love him so it doesn't matter to me."

Marybeth nodded, she didn't understand but she knew Chrys would tell her it was because she was young. Truth be told though, so was Chrys.

"Okay, here see her nose was bleeding." Carne said bringing Belinda out.

"It's nothing Lindy. Really so I got a nose bleed, what's new?" said Chrys taking them off to the side out of earshot.

"Caren they're common place in cancer patients." Belinda told her dismissing it as nothing with a wave of her hand.

"Not when they haven't had their chemo that day or the day before." Caren told her. Sometimes she wondered how she kept track of what she did, Caren didn't have that kind of access.

"Why haven't you been taking chemo?" Belinda asked.

"It's worse than before. It hurts more and I get sicker than before. It's just different." she told them.

"Okay, that's it. We're going to an x-ray of that head of yours." Belinda told her

Chrys laughed "No, I'm sane. Promise."

"We are how ever going to get a CAT scan. To be safe." She said and Chrys groaned

"I hate those stupid things!"

"Yea, I know but to be safe." Belinda told her as they walked to the elevator. Going up Chrys suddenly got dizzy. She held on to the wall even when they stopped moving. When she stepped out the rush of air made her feel nauseous. She puked violently right in the hallway.

"Okay, here we go." Belinda said "This really isn't normal."

"I've thrown up before." Chrys told her as she washed her face off, preparing for the CAT scan.

"No, when you haven't had chemo. Especially not at that rate of chemo." Belinda told her "You had to go down to levels, darling. Your dosage is much lower."

Chrys laid down for the scan holding still when she felt the same nauseous feeling only much less intense. She held it together for the 5 minutes she was in there, but the second she was let out of the chamber it spewed all over.

"Sorry." Chrys whispered as she was led back to her room. Where Kalvin was waiting, informed of what was happening. Surprisingly he was calm. He walked over, picked her up and set her gently in the bed. She fell asleep soon after. Him right by her side. At that point, Frank walked in.

"Hey." he whispered.

"Hey." Kalvin responded

"How is she?" Frank asked setting 'I'm sorry I've been away for so long flowers' on the desk.

"I don't know, dude. I guess they did some fancy scan thing. And something is wrong. I don't know."

Frank too was surprised at how well he was taking it. He just patted his friends shoulder and said

"She's fine." Sitting down he added "She'll be fine."

Kalvin smiled a half smile. He didn't believe him but he was exhausted. He couldn't be angry or sad anymore. He just was.

Chrys coughed waking up asking "What happened?"

"You got sick." Kalvin told her taking her hand "Frank's here."

"Really?" she asked sitting up.

"Yea, sorry." Frank said handing her the flowers

"It's fine." She said hugging him.

"They did some test?" Frank asked and Chrys explained.

A few hours later Belinda came back in. Her face gleaming.

"Baby girl pack your bags!" she said loudly

"What? Why? Where am I going, this is the only cancer wing?" Chrys asked and Kalvin stood. Frank sitting, looked puzzled.

"Baby, you are cancer free! You have a little radiation poisoning but, no cancer!" she said smiling. "This time for sure!"

"How?" Chrys asked

"You mustn't have had it when you came her. We did the test but I-I guess they were wrong." Belinda said showing her the CAT scan. The scan showed scar tissue damage.

"That's from after you heeled." Belinda explained.

Mostly it was a hunch that it was gone forever. On that hunch, they brought in scientist who specialized in curing cancer. Chrys told them about the berries and the guck. Surprisingly they wanted them to take them to the berries and guck. Chrys chartered a plane and she and Kalvin were to take the scientists there. However, there was trouble brewing they knew nothing of. The island was in multiple countries air space. Without, Chrys and Kalvin's knowledge Frank and the twins arranged for the island to be bought from those countries and placed in Chrys and Kalvin's names. All this was done while they were on the way to the island.

"There it is!" Chrys exclaimed as the island came within sight. It wasn't a very long trip. They got word that the island was now owned by Kalvin and Chrys whom allowed the scientists to set up a laboratory on the island. They brought in engineers, architects, and contractors by the dozen. It was done within two months. Chrys told them it was to remain the only developed thing on their island, which they promptly named Robinson Island. They allowed for a small airstrip to be built along with a hut as their airport. Chrys went through the trials and decided it would be a Democracy. With alliances with The USA, Canada, England and multiple other countries. However, everything they needed would be made on their island or in America. There was no real currency, all their money was expected to come from the laboratory.

"I don't feel right charging to live." Chrys said to Kalvin on their way back to the US one day.

"What do you mean?" he asked

"Well, not everyone will be able to afford the BLG Cure." (BLG- berry, leaf, guck) she explained.

She had refused to let Caren and Eric pay for his treatment. The cure to cancer, she couldn't believe it. She knew she said that something good would come of them being on the island but she never expected that. She never expected her life to get back to 'normal' and truthfully she didn't want it to. So when she found out she owned the island, with Kal, she was ecstatic. Normal just on her agenda. She wanted to be different, and now she could be. She owned an island, where she would live and someday so would other people. It would be an elite few who got to live there. A clan, she called them. She wasn't sure who it would be, but, she would find out soon enough. She was to hold interviews. The only method of communication was through the airport, the only place allowed to have electricity and basic cable. The animal, and plant, populations were to be carefully monitored and all killings done humanely. Chrys was not about to let place fall into, what she called, a state of Americanism. Though an American herself, she knew the country needed major help. There would be no toleration for prejudice, it would be ground for removal from the island, banishment to be exact. Horse and buggy, or boat, would be their method of transportation. Crime was not to be tolerated. All decisions would be made by Chrys or Kalvin and an impartial party from one country or another that they were allies with. But first, the unveiling of the man who discovered the cure to cancer. Also the unveiling of the Astrvski Falls, named for the three brothers who saved them.

And her animals, found her almost immediately. The wolf, now dog like, ran up and licked her face. The horse, Zephyr, followed, trailed by his more reluctant family soon named Peureux, which was German for timid, and their son BraveHeart, named so for the arrow-shooting-a-heart like scar on his behind. The bird, Pookie II and monkey, Rosie, soon followed. The twins were to be moved out there as soon as possible. Her animals, Pookie the twins' bird and Kaliana her Alaskan-Malamute Husky Mix, from her house were to be sent over with her sisters. Frank was to stay in America until a hut was made (with a bridge to Chrys and Kalvin's).

Upon their arrival back in the USA, Chrys and Kalvin were treated to a media frenzy. Apparently two teenagers running a country was important news. Even more so than the cure to cancer, which no one understood. They were seated in a press conference room as soon as possible and bombarded with questions. None of which they answered, they waited a few minutes for them to keep asking. Eventually they all quieted down when they got the message.

"Thank you." Chrys said softly. "I know you all have questions, but I have to say some things before hand."

"First yes I am officially cancer free. Second yes Robinson Island is an official country and no it is not open for anyone to move there. There will be interviews and we will pick whom will live there with us. Third we will be making some major announcements about the island momentarily. You may ask your questions now, one by one in an orderly fashion, like adults."

"Your too good at this." Kal whispered

"You've met my parents, they're roving media hogs."

He smiled and the first man asked his question "Is it true that they two of you are engaged?"

"Yes." Chrys answered

"Is it true that you are going to charge for treatment."

"Partly." Chrys answered while whispering to Kalvin "Short bursts, they're apt to ask and listen if you do."

"What does that mean?" the reports all asked at once

"It means that those with significant funds will be charge and those without will not be."

"Why?"

"Because we need to fund the production and they have money. It would be unfair to limit treatment to those with money." Chrys explained.

"You have money."

"And I paid!" Chrys said defensively. "While the five-year-old little boy at my hospital whose family could not have afforded it got it for free, does it now seem fair?"

"Okay. Enough!" Kalvin spoke up then "We are not here to defend our actions, we decided this is what's right now deal with it!" It was a spur of the moment decision but they knew it was the right one.

"Subtle." Chrys laughed "Okay, now for the announcements!" she stood up and walked over to a podium, where a screen stood silent, ready for her to play. She clicked ON and then PLAY. Pictures began rolling by of the BLG Cure and the scientist and Chrys and Kalvin on the island with them. All of the above-mentioned happenings there scrolled by.

"This is our island. Robinson Island. Named after the book The Swiss Family Robinson ©, which gave us our idea to build huts." She began "This is the laboratory the manufactures, in a green manner, a compact version of BLG cure. The only change is it is packed for transportation, nothing is added or subtracted. Trust me, if we changed it, it wouldn't and if it didn't work, I wouldn't be here." Kalvin nodded, now okay with the subject, "This is the original and now here is the finished. See practically the same, just you know more compact."

"Okay, out first announcement is that the official discoverer of the cure for cancer has been named. His name is Kalvin Vance." Kalvin stood shocked

"Oh, yeah." Chrys laughed "He didn't know they named him as the man who discovered the cure for cancer, even though he did. So who else would they name?" Pictures were taken and statement, and then Chrys and Kalvin stood near the podium.

"Our second announcement, though pale in comparison from societies view. Is important to us. We figured the men who saved us deserved to be memorialized on the island. As does BLG. So the swamp-forest area where BLG grows in now officially BLG Forest. More importantly the waterfall, near our hut is now" Chrys clicked the slide show forward to show the waterfall "Astrvski Falls! Named for the courageous and dedicated men who rescued us, Vincent, Nicoli and Derk Astrvski! Come on up here guys!" she waved them up, she had asked them there but refused to tell them why. They came up blushing, shook hands and had their pictures and statement taken again.

They returned the next day to the hospital for a final check up/ goodbye.

"If any of you want to come live with us on our island the answer will always be yes. We could use some doctors you know." Chrys told them after saying final good-byes. She waved then and walked out the door. The interviews were later that day and then they were set to depart.

They set up a make shirt office in a parking lot of a local grocery store. They had people lining up. Eventually after a rigorous questioning and background check along with a long elimination process they settled on 3 families, 2 single people, and two couples. With room for Frank and his future family, and the girls from the hospital and one surprise guest. The families consisted of a gay Caucasian couple, remember no prejudice, and their adopted seven-month-old Asian son. An African American couple and their three daughters ages ranging from 3 to16. A Hispanic couple with their two sons and one daughter, ages from newborn to 5. The single people consist of an Asian man and Middle Eastern woman. And the two couples consisted of a mixed race young couple and an elderly mixed race couple. The races were not part of the process by which they were chosen, it was just an odd coincidence that they covered the whole span.

Their mystery guest was none other than Lela. She had recently been receiving counseling and had been attempting to reconcile with Sammy and Jennie.

They arrived at the island, thinking they were going to have to build the huts only to find that they construction workers had taken it upon themselves to build them in the same fashion Chrys had and were prepared to make changes to accommodate their future residence. Whom were to arrive in a months' time. While Kalvin busied himself with the construction and what not commenting "Gotta stay in shape." Chrys laughed thinking *if that's out of shape, in shape must be crazy!* All she said aloud was

"Okay, I'm gonna go check the airstrip out." And she kissed his cheek, walking away with her 'dog' Trek (aka the wolf) at her side. She walked for a while humming to herself and petting her 'puppy' as she called him.

"Trek, I wonder what your story is sometimes. I wonder where you came from and what you've been through. But, then I realize that my story doesn't matter to you, you only know now. I kinda wonder what that's like." She laughed and petted his head. "I'm talking to a wolf, that's nice."

She ended up at the airstrip, momentarily forgetting why she came. She wandered inside turning on the news. Headlines read 'LOST KIDS CURE CANCER....' She laughed thinking *Wow, finally! Geez, you would think even American's wouldn't be so self absorbed at to put cancer behind celebrity gossip...* She really began to wonder why the news had taken so long to reach them, then seeing the date on the corner of the screen, weeks behind, realized they needed to update the cable. Writing a note and placing it on the screen, she wondered further into the office. Pictures covered the walls along with framed newspaper articles. She picked up the phone instinctively dialing Frank's number. He picked up panting.

"Bad time?" Chrys asked laughing.

"Chrys! No, just out running." He said from the other end. He stopped running and plopped himself down on the side of the road.

"Oh." Chrys answered.

"Something wrong?" he asked lying in the grass.

"No, just miss you, that's all." She told him sitting on a desk.

He laughed "I miss you too, sis." He'd taken to calling her that.

"Things aren't ever going to be normal again huh?" Chrys asked.

"Normal, when were they?" Frank asked laughing, he stopped and asked "Chrys, are you sure everything is okay? Something happen with Kal?"

"No, that's not it. When are you coming?"

"Soon, Chrys soon. You can tell me you know whatever it is."

"I know. I know." She said smiling and sighing "It's just that I promised Kal that when we were back I'd find his sister for him and then it turned into all about me again. It always is. I feel like you're always left in the background and I feel bad."

"Chrys, I'm not in the background. Really."

"I just don't want you to feel replaced."

"Replaced? Is that what this is about? No, Chrys I get it, you love him. It's not replacement. You'll always be my best friend."

"You're my best friend too, forever."

"I know."

It was silent for a few moments "I can find his sister, if you want?"

"No, I couldn't ask you to do that."

"Well, too bad I'm going to anyway."

Chrys laughed, "I want to hug you right now, that's the first thing you have to do when you get here. That's an order."

"Oh, really?" Frank laughed.

"Really." Chrys said smiling. "I have to go now, call you in a few days?"

"Yeah." He said softly "Love ya, sis."

"Love you too."

She hung up then. Walking back out into the main lobby area Chrys sat down, leaning his head on Trek's side. She laid there for a while until Kalvin came running in. She sat up and he sat near her.

"Chrys what are you doing here?" he asked as she leaned on him.

"I don't know." She said silent tears slipping from her eyes.

"Chrys, what's wrong?" Kalvin asked slipping his arms around her.

"I-I didn't find your sister." She said crying into his chest. He laughed and ran his hands down her hair.

"Chrys, hon, it's okay."

"But- but I promised. And-and now because of me you're living here away from everyone."

"Chrys, hon, you are my everyone. And everyone else will be here soon. I know you miss your sisters. And I know you miss Frank. But, they're not gone forever just for now." He told her kissing the top of her head. "Look at me. Chrys, it will all be okay. I love you, they love you. If they didn't would they want to come back? We all *wanted* to come back as much as you did."

"But..."

"But, nothing. My sister isn't a big priority, okay. I know you feel bad because you say you promised, but it's okay. She doesn't want anything to do with me. That's not your fault, it's mine. It's not your problem, okay?"

"Who are you?" Chrys asked laughed "And what have you done with Kalvin?"

He kissed her head and laid back on his elbows. She laid her head on his chest and Trek came over, licked her face and laid at her feet.

"Kal, when do you want to get married?"

"Whenever you want to." She looked at him, "Seriously, if I didn't want to marry you I wouldn't have asked."

She hugged him "I know, but we can't do it here, we have to go to America. It seems like a lot of trouble. Maybe we should move a priest, or whatever, here."

"We could do that, and then all of the people here, and Frank and your sisters, could be the guests."

"I want the girls from the hospital to come."

"We can do that."

Chrys closed her eyes and fell asleep soon after. It wasn't late she was just tired. Kalvin fell asleep not long after. They slept there throughout the night, curled around each other, Trek at their feet.

****

The plane landed, the very first plane to land on their landing strip, and the people emerged. The plane took off and a second landed. Their group pictures were taken and hung in the office. Chrys ran out, jumped into Frank's arms crying. He set her down kissed her forehead. She hugged him again and then her sisters ran to her squeezing her and crying. She hugged and kissed them. Then as they stepped aside, saying hi and hugging Kalvin, Frank led Sammy and Jennie up to Kalvin. Chrys cried dropping to the ground, hugging them.

"How did you-" Chrys began crying so uncontrollably she couldn't finish. She stood up throwing her arms around Frank, he rubbed her back, and Kalvin laughed. She let go for a moment and then grasped back onto Frank. She eventually let go and led the group to their huts telling them all she thought they needed to know. After all was said and done she walked back over to her hut and climbed up, exhausted. Her puppy Kaliana came bounding toward her licking her face, Trek growled jealously from the corner.

"Shh, Trek, this is Kaliana, be friends." She said patting his head and her puppy's.

"Chrys?" Kalvin called from the 'moon roof' as Chrys called it. It was really a platform built onto their roof, which let in the night sky through a moveable portion of the storm cover.

"Yea, I'm coming!" she called climbing up. She found all those who had originally inhabited the island with her. She smiled settling down between Kalvin and Frank, grabbing Frank's hand and leaning on Kalvin. They all set there until the moon began to lower in the sky and those younger slept soundly. Carrying them down they returned to the roof.

"Frank?" Chrys said as they sat there.

"Yeah?" he answered

"I don't know." She replied after a moment laughing and smiling.

"Chrys don't worry. I love it here; I wanted to come back too. Don't worry." She looked at him and smiled, he always knew what she was thinking.

"I tried to tell you that." Kalvin chimed in.

"I know." She said playfully pushing him.

"Well, night y'all. It's my last night in this hut so I think I'll sleep part of it" Frank laughed kissing Chrys's head "Night sis love ya. Night Kal."

"Night, dude." Kal said.

"Kal" Chrys said after he left.

"Yea?" he asked looking at her, she was crying "What's wrong?"

She scotched over curling up close to him. He ran his hand down her back, she closed her eyes.

"Nothing, just letting it all come out I guess." She told him, not moving from her position. She closed her eyes. Despite him being a guy and embodying everything a guy embodies he never got annoyed or angry with her emotions. He never got annoyed with her at all.

"That's good." He told her smiling. She sat up looking at him he laid back closing his eyes. She crawled up as close to him as she could get. There was a love, and there would always be a love, as strong and passionate and true, as it was when they arrived at the island. There was just less heartache. Of course they all knew that there would be heartache in life, but for now things were peaceful.

****

Chrys woke up the next morning to find Kalvin bringing back kindling for the fire the twins and Frank had going. She climbed down from the moon roof and sat near her sisters. She hugged each of them, still tired. Sammy came bounding out of her room throwing herself at Chrys. Chrys hugged her, the little girl settling down into her lap. Jennie came toddling out next and Marianne scooped her up, setting down with her. They ate breakfast, settling back into their chores.

"Chrys, come here." Frank whispered as Chrys was walking back from tending to the barn animals. She walked over to him.

"Yea?" she asked filling her pail with water again.

"I found her." He said smiling a broad proud smile.

"Who?" Chrys inquired confused.

"Kal's sister." She must have looked shocked because he laughed.

"Really?!" she asked and he nodded, she threw her arms around his neck kissing his cheek. She ran to where she knew Kalvin would be, with the construction crew. He always was. It was the only real exercise place on the island. He contemplated building one, but wasn't sure. What he didn't know was that she already had told the construction crew to build him one. What she didn't know was that he had a children's home/hut built near the ocean along with a chapel. He also a priest on the way there. He let her plan her wedding telling her 'don't worry I'll take care of the preacher and the place' and she let him.

"Kalvin! Kalvin!!" she shouted.

"Yeah? Is everything alright?" he asked running over to you.

"Frank- Frank she panted found your sister." Her face was beaming and his stood stony. "Aren't you happy?" she asked her smile fading.

"I-I don't know." He said and she saw she might have opened up a wound he wanted to keep closed.

"Oh, I'm sorry I should've asked you first. I just wanted to make you happy." She told him. He nodded, he knew that. He just wasn't sure if he wanted go back there. She resembled everything he was running from. He left his sister and the gang at the same time.

"What-what did she say?" he asked

"I-I don't know I didn't stay and ask. I ran right over here to you." She said taking his hand and walking slowly back. They walked over to Frank and Kalvin just stood there, silent. Chrys was scared but just squeezed his hand and whispered "Ask."

He just stood there squeezing her hand harder, his head down.

She took the lead "Tell *us* everything." She emphasized us, to let him know he wasn't alone. He got the message. He couldn't be alone, never with her there and that was exactly how he liked it. He knew she would always be there for him.

"I searched through every phone book I could get my hands on and went to your old neighborhood. Everything, and I found nothing. So I decided to put up posters with her name on them and my phone number. And she called it. So I told her who I was and why I called. I told her how you changed. She was angry at first, she didn't want anything to do with me or you." Noting the look on his face Frank paused and Chrys leaned her head on his arm.

"But, she called back a few days later, asking questions. A little- tentative- but she wanted to know how you were and all that. Eventually I convinced her to come here and talk to you... tomorrow."

"T-tomorrow?" he stuttered.

"Shh, it's okay." Chrys said leading him away mouthing to Frank 'Thank you. Thank you so much.' Frank nodded unsure if he did the right thing. Chrys was sure though, she knew it needed to be done and if not then when?

"Chrys." Kalvin said as they sat down on the moon roof "I-I can't do this."

"Oh, shh, yes you can. So it's scary. Everybody gets scared. All you have to do is be yourself." Chrys told him rubbing her hands up and down his arm and chest. He sat there nodding.

****

The plane landed and Kalvin's heart was beating, his hand clenched Chrys's. He closed his eyes as the doors opened. Chrys pulled him closer, he opened his eyes and there she was just as he left her.

Kameron sat in her chair staring at him with her deep blue eyes, their only difference her long black hair braided and hung over her shoulder. Kalvin's mother once told him, right after the drive by, 'You were born with blue eyes, just like your sisters. By the time you were seven they were gray. Now so is your soul.' His breathing was heavy as Chrys let go of his hand and stepped back, he looked behind him and she smiled motioning wither hands to go, go forward.

"You look the same." Kameron told him, "When people change, so do their looks."

"No," Kalvin said slowly "not always."

"You always did." Kameron said, both their minds flashing to what their mom said.

"Have you ever seen a baby picture of me?" he asking confronting his mom's statement. "I've always had gray eyes."

"And your soul?" his sister asked bitterly.

He smiled because he knew the answer to that one. For once in his life he really knew he had changed, he really knew who he was.

"It changed a few times. It's been gray, blue, red, black but now..." he paused looking back at Chrys who smiled at him hopefully "now it's white."

"White?" Kameron asked

"Clean. New. White." Kalvin told her.

She paused "I don't get you."

"Because you don't know me, the real me. But, I don't know you either. So, I guess the only thing left to say is do you want to do about it?"

119

She sat there thinking for a moment. "Is that your girlfriend?"

"Fiancé." He corrected her.

"And him?" she asked slightly shocked.

"Her best friend...my best friend."

"What have they done?" she asked. It took him a moment to figure out what she meant.

"Frank, drugs. Chrys, leukemia."

Kameron stopped, she was sick and he was still marrying her? Then it dawned on her, she was cured.

"Your too much. For a moment I really believed that you changed. I really thought 'wow he really is different. She's dying and he still wants to marry her' but you found the cure. That doesn't make you a good man."

Kalvin nodded, looking down.

"Okay, stop!" Chrys said forcefully, walking up to Kameron. "Just stop! You do *not* know him, okay? He loved me when I was sick and now! He asked to marry me before the cure!" she stopped there the look on Kameron's face said it all.

She went to their hut with them, Marianne and Marybeth waiting at the door. They ran down.

"Chrys, Kalvin. Hurry it's Jennie!" they said in unison as they all ran up then, Kalvin pausing picking his sister up and carrying her up with him. He set her on the floor and ran into Sammy and Jennie's room. The little girl was bleeding from her head and screaming in pain. Chrys picked her up, cradling her in her arms. Kissing the little girl and crying. Kalvin ran out practically jumping down from their hut and running as fast as he could to every hut until he found the doctor. They had allowed one of the scientists, whom was also a doctor, to live there.

"Please," he said heaving from running "It's-it's my daughter." Daughter, it just happened, he hadn't meant to say it and he hadn't thought about it. They ran back and the doctor took Jennie. Kalvin held Chrys as she cried, holding Sammy in her arms. The young girl cried into Chrys's chest as she whispered words of comfort. Kalvin held Chrys and Kameron sat there shocked, watching how he closed his eyes and whispered a silent prayer. Kameron gasped silently to herself when the single silent tear slipped from her brothers' eye. She had never seen him cry, she'd never seen him care about anything. The doctor came back a half an hour later.

"She'll be fine. She had a nasty concussion but other than that she'll be just fine." Chrys let out a relieved cry hugging Sammy closer to her. Kalvin squeezed them both close, kissing Chrys's head and shaking the doctor's hand.

"Thank you so much. Thank you." Chrys said hugging the doctor, Kalvin nodded the doctor left then, saying he would keep Jennie to monitor for the night. Chrys walked away then, carrying Sammy. Holding Marianne by the hand, Marybeth holding Sammy's hand. Chrys remained in there with them for the night.

"Kalvin." Kameron said as he headed down the ladder. He returned in a minutes carrying her chair. He set her in it, silently and sat by the fire.

"Do you want to stay?" he asked her eventually

"What?" she asked

"Do you want to stay?" he repeated "I need to know, so I can build a ramp."

"I'm not sure." She told him

"I'll build one anyway." He told her, after a moment, a long pause he spoke again "I'm sorry, Kammie. I really am. I never meant it."

"I know. I always knew that. I was just mad. It will take me time, K, to fully move on. To know the real you."

"I know, took me time too."

"Tell me about your life." She asked, slipping down from her chair next to him.

"Chrys, my fiancé. Frank, my best friend. Marianne and Marybeth, Chrys's sisters. They're twins, like us. And they fight, like us." Kameron smiled at that. "Sammy and Jennie, my-" he paused "my daughters. They trusted from the beginning. Looks or past, which they will know, they won't care."

"I've never seen you love or care about anything."

"I have though, cared. I care about you and mom."

"Mom loves you, she always has. She was scared and angry."

"I know."

"She sent this. When I told her you had kids, cause your friend um, Frank, I think it is, yeah, he told me about them." Kameron handed him a package. He opened it and inside was a letter, a very long letter from his mother. And a photo album, with the words, "To Sammy and Jennie. Love Gramma." He smiled and opened it. It contained pictures of him and his mother and Kameron. There were blank pages. He opened to one, pulled out his wallet and slipped a picture of Chrys into it. Kameron smiled,

"Do you have pictures of the rest of them?"

He shook his head no "I have a camera though."

"Good, we can take pictures." And that is exactly what they did. The next day Kameron set out, taking pictures of all of them together, including Jennie. Individual pictures. And pictures of each of them with the rest, such as Kalvin with Chrys, then with Frank, etc. Printing them all at the airport and slipping them into the photo album. Chrys took pictures of all their animals, slipping them in too. Chrys took a picture of Kalvin and his sister, pausing for a moment to look at it slipped it in too. She handed it to Sammy and Jennie telling them

"This is your family. Never forget that." She picked up Jennie and kissed her head, walking out into the living room. Sammy staying to look through the picture album.

****

Kalvin read his mothers letter and re-read it. He wrote her and that is how they rebuilt they're relationship. He wrote of his life there and his friends and Chrys. He wrote of his sisters-in-law-to-be and he wrote of his daughters. And his daughters they were. Officially they became so two months after Kameron's arrival via adoption through the US. You never saw Chrys happier. Although she was always happy, for the most part. That day Chrys held Jennie in her arms, kissed her head, bent down and kissed Sammy's head. Whispering 'My daughters, my babies.' Kalvin picked Sammy up, she hugged him, kissed Jennie and they all smiled, holding up the paper stating they were a family as Kameron took their picture.

****

Their marriage with the preacher and the makeshift church was beautiful. It was small and it was happy. Flowers lined the pews and the residence sat in their church clothes as the young couple said their vows. Frank the best man, Kameron the maid of honor. Marianne and Marybeth bride's maids. Sammy the flower girl and Jennie the ring bearer. Chrys walked in her white dress, her KC necklace shining off of her chest, Kalvin's KC ring placed diligently on his right hand. They smiled at each other, Chrys was shaking. Kalvin took her hands in his. Tears poured from her eyes as the little wedding in their hut became real, the little vows became longer and the meaning remained the same.

Chrys looked all around her that day, watching everyone she loved smile. Watching her new friends smile for her. Everything felt whole, everything felt right. Nothing more or nothing less, everything was perfect. She new for once in her life that everything and everyone would be alright. She was finally where she needed to be with who she needed to be with. She smiled, secretly thanking leukemia for what it gave her. Without it she wouldn't be where she was. She knew she owed everything to it, so she would forever be grateful. But, now, now was time to be happy and happy she was. She smiled and laughed and danced at her dream wedding with her dream man. And their perfectly imperfect life.

****

2 YEARS LATER

Perfectly imperfect it was. Their life remained simple and strange on that island. Little by little there be no more cancer. They lived quietly, peaceful out of the American media's prying eye. Frank found love in the eldest daughter, Tia, of the African American couple living on the island. Kameron returned to the US to live with her mother, writing and calling her brother. Their relationships repaired. Kalvin finally knew what Chrys meant when she said 'You can come from any place in the world, that place does not define you. What you do with it, does.' Marianne and Marybeth, now teens of 13, attended a boarding school in America, where all the island children went while they set up the island school. Boarding school was hard for all involved but the school was almost finished on the island and the teachers were almost all there, to remain in a hotel like thing for the school year, and most returned to their homes in the US, some lived on the island. They returned every summer to live with their sister, who attempted, inspired by Kalvin to mend broken relationships with her parents. Chrys remained Chrys, tending with diligence to her children and animals. Her animals, Zephyr, Peureux and BraveHeart added a wild bundle of joy to their family. Sweet little Pea came without warning. Pookie and Pookie II ran and flew around together, the exceedingly larger Pookie II would often be caught with Pookie on her back. Rosey, the little monkey, grew into a bright adolescent, eager for adventure, accompanying Jennie everywhere and Sammy too, when she was home from school. The ever faithful Trek soon found his mate in Kaliana, the two of them adding four little mouths to the family. Maia, Jack, Matia and Jessup. Jack and Jessup were wild and brave their sisters Maia and Matia more refined, smart little girls.

Sammy and Jennie were happy loved little girls. It didn't take them long to call Chrys and Kalvin mommy and daddy. And it didn't take them long to put their hands on Chrys's stomach and talk to their baby brother. Their baby brother, Cannon, whom would make his entrance to the little island world, with dark hair, black as his fathers and bright hazel eyes.

Life was smooth for them, comparably to what life used to be. They were happy in their strange perfectly imperfect little world. So I guess, they lived happily ever after.

The End

Filename: Lost
Directory: C:\Users\Owner\Documents
Template: C:\Users\Owner\AppData\Roaming\Microsoft\Templates\Normal.dotm
Title:
Subject:
Author: Janie May Phillips
Keywords:
Comments:
Creation Date: 10/3/2010 4:57:00 PM
Change Number: 321
Last Saved On: 10/9/2011 8:58:00 PM
Last Saved By: Kadi Mae Spear
Total Editing Time: 60,974 Minutes
Last Printed On: 11/2/2011 5:20:00 PM
As of Last Complete Printing
    Number of Pages: 125
    Number of Words: 33,802 (approx.)
    Number of Characters: 192,676 (approx.)

Zeitfracht Medien GmbH
Ferdinand-Jühlke-Straße 7
99095 Erfurt, Deutschland
produktsicherheit@kolibri360.de

Druck:
CPI Druckdienstleistungen GmbH
im Auftrag der
Zeitfracht Medien GmbH
Ein Unternehmen der Zeitfracht - Gruppe
Ferdinand-Jühlke-Str. 7
99095 Erfurt